"I NEVER WANT TO OWN YOU," HE RETORTED, "ONLY TO POSSESS YOU."

"Go to hell!" A hot, bright color flushed her skin. Suddenly the music stopped. The dance had ended. Cathy tried to push away from him, but he held her and would not let go. "My uncle was right about you, Derek Guenther!" she whispered, furious. "You're a swine. Always were and always will be."

His eyes glittered in cold amusement. Suddenly, before she realized what he was about to do, and certainly before she could have done anything to stop him, he claimed her with a hard and angry kiss that left her weak with desire...

RAPTURE REGAINED

SERENA
ALEXANDER

A JOVE BOOK

First Jove edition published August 1981

First printing

"Second Chance at Love" and the butterfly emblem are trademarks be-
longing to Jove Publications, Inc.

Printed in the United States of America

Jove books are published by Jove Publications, Inc.,
200 Madison Avenue, New York, NY 10016

RAPTURE REGAINED

chapter 1

AS SHE WALKED away from her overheated Land-Rover, Cathy Dawson glanced up at the dark clouds gathered in the sky, then sniffed the moisture-laden air. She stopped, standing as still as a statue, and listened to the birds squawking. Normally throaty and melodious, their cries had turned shrill, coming louder and faster in an urgent cascade of storm warnings. Far off a dog barked. Carried on currents of electrified air, his yelping sounded uncannily clear.

Turning in a slow, unconsciously graceful pirouette, Cathy scanned the distant mountain peak that marked the boundary of her vision. She had spent her earliest years here in Malawi, leaving unwillingly when her parents had taken her back to America at age ten. Having always regarded Tanyasi, the private wildlife preserve owned by her uncle, as her true home, she had returned to this haven during the ugly, painful months when her parents were getting a divorce. And here, at age twenty, Cathy had found herself involved with a man only a few months older than herself, whose love and passion had been overwhelming, whose betrayal had left her shattered, afraid ever again to trust anyone as she had trusted him, afraid to love without wariness.

She'd vowed never to return to Tanyasi, but she hadn't anticipated her uncle's failing health. Without help he would have to sell his beloved Africa House and move into Blantyre, Malawi's largest city.

Unable to stand the idea of strangers taking over, Cathy had quit her job in the States and come back to Malawi. But not without misgivings. Running her uncle's estate was on the positive side, then there was the negative. And in the three days since her return, she'd found that what she feared was true—every place in this beautiful land was filled with memories that should have been buried and put to rest long before. To purge these ghosts, or at least to try, Cathy had borrowed one of her uncle's Land-Rovers and had driven alone into the bush.

Derek Guenther—his memory, his very presence, though long vanished from her life—haunted her. As she passed an abandoned native hut, cone-shaped and thatched with mud and reed, she relived again that

stunning, amazing hour six years ago when the two
of them had lain in one another's arms for the first
time. On that sunny February afternoon she had
learned what it truly meant to be a woman. The sensation of Derek's warm lips pressing hers and of his
lean, tanned arms around her rushed back. A warm,
sensual, and totally unwanted feeling washed over her.

She remembered their wild, dust-raising rides to
secret places where two who loved could be alone to
express their shared desires. Then she remembered
that last terrible day when their car had gone off the
road and overturned. She had awakened in traction
hours later in a hospital in Blantyre, and from that
afternoon on she had wondered why he had not waited
with her, had not helped her, and had never shown his
face again in her life. Even now the bewilderment, the
misery, was not entirely gone. Why, she wondered,
when she had given him so much, had he given back
so little? He had claimed to love her, yet his actions
had proven otherwise. Shaking herself, Cathy tried to
beat the memories down, to send them back again to
her subconscious.

She forced herself to turn her attention to the scene
around her, hoping that Malawi would again work its
magic for her. She was not disappointed. As it had in
the past, the countryside she loved so well helped her
forget painful memories, and her old love for this
rugged land rose up in her again.

In east central Africa, Malawi was a place of stunning contrasts where dramatic highlands jutted sky-
ward, mirrored in the waters of shimmering lakes.

From one of these, an inland sea called Lake Nyasa, poured the Shire River, a great silver ribbon that flowed close to the borders of her uncle's estate and southward into Mozambique. But now, over all this incredible landscape, black clouds were billowing and swelling. Cathy knew they would erupt in a few short hours into the first rainfall ending the dry season. It seemed to her that it might storm. She frowned, a little worried, and glanced uneasily at her Land-Rover in the middle of the dirt service road. She knew she'd have to wait longer for its wretched engine to cool, and she moved off through thigh-high grasses, brown and dry from weeks of drought. They rustled and crackled as she went through them on her aimless exploration. She sighed, exasperated with the situation.

Because the day had started out hot and muggy, she'd scraped her hair away from her face. The thick blue-black hair, inherited from her Cree Indian grandmother, was parted in the middle, then woven into tight braids fastened like a tiara close around her head. A few tendrils around the hairline had worked free, though, and the rising wind lifted and teased them.

She turned at the sound of hooves. Not twenty yards away a small herd of eland, the largest of the African antelope, pounded past a stand of trees. At once Cathy felt a pang. At the same time she blessed fortune that Tanyasi existed as it did. Not only antelopes, but buffalo, great cats, elephants and zebras, too, lived on Tanyasi's acres. Her Uncle Howard, a romantic, loved animals and had been ahead of the times. Years ago he had turned the overgrown farm he bought into a wildlife haven. He knew that only in preserves, either government-owned or private like Tanyasi, would Africa's wild creatures live on, protected by caring people from other humans . . . and their encroaching "civilization." Cathy, too, was devoted to wildlife preservation. She'd often thought it was only in this love of animals and nature, which she shared with her Uncle Howard, that her American Indian heritage survived.

Heart and soul—if not in looks—Cathy knew she was typically American, though she appeared to be more southern European. What a mix! Her oval face, with its delicately aquiline nose and creamy ivory complexion that never tanned could have come from southern France or Italy. When her hair was worn up as it was today, she looked like a madonna painted upon the glowing canvas of an Italian Renaissance master.

At the moment, however, Cathy did not feel like a madonna, but like a very annoyed woman. She really hated machines that acted up on her the way the Land-Rover had. Sighing, she went toward it. Her long, black lashes flickered a little as she eyed "the monster" suspiciously. She felt that she had now given it enough time to cool. As she climbed in, adjusting the cloth that kept her back—half-bare in its halter top—from sticking against the Naugahyde upholstery, she calculated she was almost thirty miles from Africa House, the rambling Victorian mansion in the middle of Tanyasi's acres where her Uncle Howard had lived for almost twenty-five years.

Cathy's frown deepened. Before stopping, she had heard a rattle in the engine. She had hoped it would go away when she started up again, but as her foot pushed down on the gas pedal, she realized it hadn't. Even worse, the heat indicator needle leaped dangerously fast once again toward "hot." But with a storm coming, and no help in sight, she had no choice really but to keep on driving toward Africa House.

She glanced at the wind-swaying grasses. Hidden in them, she saw a lioness crouched low. The creature stalked, its amber eyes wide and intent, but Cathy could not see its prey. Feeling vulnerable, she blessed the half ton or so of metal surrounding her, protecting her from animals like that lioness. Thinking again of the engine of the Land-Rover, however, Cathy felt apprehensive. Had that funny rattle grown louder or was it only her imagination? She couldn't be sure. The change, if any, had been too gradual.

Suddenly the rattle became a funny clinking that grew louder and louder. Its din drove all other thoughts from her mind and chilled her with alarm. It had begun to sound like the noise of a child banging pans together. Something was definitely wrong! She slowed down.

But what was she to do? She knew as little as anyone could about the inner workings of engines. Even if she stopped right away, she couldn't do a thing about whatever was wrong, so she kept driving but very slowly. Silently she prayed "the monster," as she definitely decided to call the jeep now, would last at least until she was within walking distance of Africa House.

A horrible clatter shattered the air. The car swerved.

Cathy pulled it back into the middle of the road again, then eased it to a stop. Groaning aloud at her misfortune, she flung open her door and swung her long slim legs out.

"Damn!" she muttered. She moved to the hood, reached underneath to lift it, and with a sigh peered into the mess of greasy pipes and tubes, big round things and vents. At once she wondered why she had bothered. It all meant nothing to her except that now she could smell a funny kind of acrid stench like burnt oil and overstressed metal. Appalled, she wondered how badly she might have damaged one of Tanyasi's two Rovers.

So it had come to this—stranded in the wilds of a none-too-well-patrolled game preserve with a bad storm coming up. She consoled herself with the thought that if she failed to show up for dinner, her Uncle Howard and the couple who worked for him would know something had happened, and they'd come looking for her. But dinner was hours away, after sunset. They couldn't search in the dark, so she was likely to be stuck out here all night in the pouring rain. Impatient by nature, Cathy would have abandoned the Land-Rover and walked. She remembered almost at once, however, the face of that lioness—intent, hungry, and on the prowl. She thought, too, of being caught in the drenching rain promised by the clouds above and didn't find the idea appealing at all. She decided to stay right where she was in the shelter and protection of that otherwise useless half-ton metal shell. There was nothing she could do but wait.

Just then she heard the faint, low droning of an engine driving closer, closer on the hard-packed dirt road that would soon turn to mud. A cry of joy burst from her lips. Rescue! She prayed that whoever was driving along this forsaken stretch of road would continue straight toward her and not turn. The sound of the engine grew louder in the afternoon's electrified air. A late-model jeep painted bright yellow with its chrome glittering from polish and newness raced around a boulder. It speeded in her direction as if the very devil himself were after it. Cathy shouted and waved madly to flag it down.

Seeing her, the driver screeched to a halt just beyond where she stood, then backed up quickly.

"Hello!" he called. "A bit of car trouble?"

A faint thickness of his speech and his Dutch South African accent warned her first. Half-horrified, she prayed her deepest fear would prove unfounded. At the first sight of him close up, though, Cathy's breath caught in her throat.

"Derek!" She went hot and cold all at once.

The man was out of the jeep in an instant, seeming to go pale beneath his dark tan while staring in disbelief. "Cathy!" he gasped.

Cathy shook her head as if to clear her vision. Derek had matured into the most stunning man she had ever seen. He stood tall and powerfully built. Though not an ounce of fat showed on him anywhere, he had lost his boyish slenderness. His chest, broad and strong, tapered to slim but powerful-looking hips. Since he had dressed for the early day's mugginess in short-sleeved khaki shirt and walking shorts, she could see that his tan, a magnificent bronze, went all the way to his feet. Gone too were the cast-off clothes of his impoverished youth. Those khakis looked custom-made and very, very expensive. But he hadn't lost his air of wildness. His white-blond hair, his ferocious expression, made her think of some half-savage Viking of days long ago.

Time froze as Cathy stared at his face. In no way could it ever be called handsome, yet she found the craggy masculinity of his maturity incredibly attractive. His strong nose, high brow, and deeply cleft chin were somehow sharper, more impressive now. A moustache partially hid his well-shaped lips. In spite of herself Cathy tingled as she remembered how often those lips had reddened hers. A certain hardness now played around his mouth as if he had become a man accustomed to giving commands and having them obeyed without question. When his lips parted, his teeth, white and strong looking, flashed at her in startling contrast to his sun-browned skin.

His eyes were the same, yet in some subtle way they had changed. Deep and blue like Northland glacier lakes they glowed clear and intense against the deep bronze of his complexion. But now they raked her with a strange combination of hunger and contempt.

She bridled at the way he was inspecting her. She could only wait, however, strangely paralyzed. And then curiosity swelled and she studied him as intensely as he studied her. According to her uncle, Derek had callously walked away from the scene of their accident six years before. He'd left her lying unconscious in the overturned jeep and later disappeared completely into the wide world beyond Malawi. Why was he back? The local families were a close-knit lot, especially those who had been on their land for two or three generations.

Ever since she could remember, the Guenther family had been outcasts, owing, she had heard, to some scandal that had occurred long before she and Derek were born. When she had started going out with Derek those six years ago, her uncle had been appalled, even furious. Defiant, she had met Derek secretly, using a borrowed car to drive to their meeting place. Poor Uncle Howard had never suspected how far things had gone—not right up until that last afternoon she had spent with Derek. Only in the hospital with neither flowers nor visits from the one who claimed to love her did she realize how right her uncle had been to forbid her to see him.

She looked up now and into Derek's eyes. His cool, arrogant stare embarrassed, yet fascinated her, and she continued to stand rooted before him. His gaze slid down the slim, soft column of her neck. She felt the pulse in the hollow of her throat begin to hammer and instantly regretted that she had dressed so casually this morning. She had chosen her clothes because of the hot weather, of course, not for unforeseen circumstances, but still . . . The black and brown print halter was but a scrap of flimsy cotton, hiding little. Derek's eyes burned across the twin swells of her breasts, then lingered a moment at that deep and tantalizing line where they nestled together.

Cathy recoiled. For the first time she realized how vulnerable she was. There was no haven to run to nor anyone near who could help her. She felt her skin prickle as his eyes skimmed down the lean, firm lines of her belly exposed between halter top and low-slung denim cut-offs. Uneasily she glanced at his hands. Those long, elegant fingers could have belonged to a concert pianist or a surgeon. Though finely formed, they appeared powerful, too. She realized with a fluttering heart that in one swift move those smooth fingers could wrap around her skimpy halter and rip it from her breasts. Those strong arms could take her by force to possess her. And if she tried to flee, she could see by the very look of his muscled legs that he could outrun her. Her breath caught in her throat, and she stared at him wide-eyed.

He raised his eyes to her face again and met her gaze. At once, to her surprise, he smiled mockingly as if what he saw had amused rather than aroused him. Bewildered now as well as unnerved, Cathy pressed her hands together to keep them from fidgeting.

The silence between them sliced at Cathy's nerves. She glanced nervously at the sky. More clouds had gathered, the sky was ominously dark, and the moisture-laden breeze blew harder against her skin.

"I'm . . . I'm so glad you came by."

"I'm sure you are!" Derek's eyes darted from her to the unmoving hulk of her uncle's beige and black Land-Rover and back to her. His gaze wandered over her figure in silent insult to her choice of clothing. "Quite a car for the likes of you, isn't it? You were always hopeless where mechanical devices were concerned."

When she didn't respond instantly, he barreled on, his words colored with even deeper tones of scorn and amusement. "You pick a strange time and place to go on a picnic, little lady."

"Well, I wasn't about—"

He cut her off. "Maybe you should have brought your uncle along with you. At least he isn't stupid enough to get you stranded."

Cathy gulped a deep, fast breath, intending to tell him in no uncertain terms to leave her uncle out of any discussion between them. She didn't get a chance.

"May I suggest you first learn to drive and maintain the car you take out," he purred with such sarcasm-laced softness that Cathy felt her blood boil. "You of all people," he continued, "should know this is not the place to find out you don't know the first thing about wilderness survival or handling four-wheel-drive vehicles."

Cathy was fuming, barely able to resist reminding him how often six years ago she'd driven just such a jeep to meet him! She clenched her teeth. Their passion for each other was the last thing she wanted to talk about with him. If looks could kill, the expression in her green eyes would have buried him. She stood with hands on hips glaring at him and aching to sear him with a jibe. But when she actually managed to speak, the unexpectedly high and squeaky timbre of her voice mortified her.

"How dare you?" And the question was even worse than her tone because the crushing comments she'd intended to hurl at him had all vanished from her mind. "How dare you?" she gasped again. "What are you even doing here?"

Blown by the wind, more of her hair had escaped from the tiara of braids. The waving tendrils dramatically set off her ivory skin which was flushed with anger. Her cheeks held the tint of wild roses and the color quickly spread across her small, well-shaped ears. She raised her head to pin Derek with a level gaze. Her strong, well-molded chin was tilted, betraying the stubborn streak in her. Suddenly Derek laughed—and the sound made her tremble with rage.

"You always did have a temper, Cathy. I suppose it's the wild Indian in you."

"Go to hell!"

That fierce remark out, she bit her lip. This anger wouldn't do. It just wouldn't do in this situation. For long moments she struggled to master the emotion. And, then, if not casually, at least civilly she was able to speak to him again.

"Are you just passing through, Derek, or have you settled here again?"

"I'm certainly not passing through," he answered in a dangerously soft voice. "Malawi is my home and has been for most of my life. No matter how that displeases anyone or everyone else!" With an abrupt movement he turned away from her. "Well, I might as well take a look at your engine and see what's wrong. Maybe I can fix it for you right now and be on my way. Once is enough," he added cryptically before pushing past her to move with long powerful strides to the damaged vehicle.

Cathy followed. Her heart was pounding. Lord, how she hoped he could make the needed repairs so she could escape. As he bent to peer into the insides of her disabled Land-Rover, she positioned herself just across from him and tried to concentrate on the situation and not on Derek. He frowned so hard as he fooled with the engine that it was clear to her at once that the damage was serious. When he made the sort of noise a doctor might when examining a seriously ill patient, she was sure that the jeep was hopelessly immobilized.

"What exactly is the problem?"

Derek gave her a rueful smile and shook his head as if pitying her stupidity. "Didn't your uncle ever tell you, little one, that engines need oil?"

Cathy stared, not sure whether to be worried or angry at his condescending remark. "Of course I know engines need oil," she said hotly. It was one of the few things she really did know about cars. She refused, however, to admit as much to him.

"Then why did you let the damned thing run dry?" He pulled out a long, thin metal wand. "This should have shown oil up to here." He spoke like a teacher lecturing a very dull pupil as he pointed to a deeply etched line. Instead of sticky goo up to that mark, though, the whole length of the wand gleamed perfectly free of any oil at all.

She shook her head, irritated and disappointed with herself. Usually she let Raymond, her uncle's mechanic, take care of checking out the car before she drove anywhere. But this time she'd been busy with something else and she'd been in a hurry to get away from Africa House and out into the bush. Impulsively—no, foolishly she knew now—she'd simply taken off. Raymond had shouted at her as she roared away down the driveway. She winced, realizing the poor man must have been trying to stop her, trying to tell her either that the oil was low or perhaps that he was going to change it in this particular vehicle.

"See this?" Derek's voice was loud and demanding.

Cathy edged around the jeep so she could see where he pointed. There was a gaping hole in the side of the engine. He began to explain what had happened, but as she couldn't understand much of what he said, her thoughts drifted away, first back to Africa House and at last back to the overwhelmingly attractive man who was lecturing her. Then Derek's booming words intruded.

"Damn it, you haven't paid attention to anything I've said," he accused. His eyes flashed fire and Cathy stepped back with a start. His emotion almost frightened her.

He continued, still angrily. "I've been trying to explain to you this stupid thing you did and what it means and you just stand there nodding as if you're listening but really lost in a little dream world of your own. What a waste of time!"

Startled by this outburst, she raised her gaze to his. At once an inner voice scolded her for allowing him to get away with such rude treatment. She was furious

that he had succeeded in intimidating—and attract-
ing—her. "Well, what do you expect?" she cried.
"You throw all that technical nonsense at me and expect me to understand? I'm not a garage mechanic,
you know."

"No, obviously not." He gave a half-disgusted
snort. "So why *am* I wasting my time?" He glanced
to the engine, then turned to her again. "In terms
simple enough even for you to understand, you burned
up your engine. You totaled it just as surely as if you
had run into a tree at sixty miles an hour. The whole
thing will have to be rebuilt."

"Oh, no!" Another problem to deal with—one of
many, but more critical than most. Howard would
have to be told. She felt a pang of dread at having to
add more to the already terrible burden of her old
uncle's declining health.

At the sight of her gazing up at him, her eyes wide
with uncertainty, he drew back. "Well, it's a nasty
situation for sure." He glanced at her car. "You'll have
to have it towed and I don't have a tow bar with me."
He softened slightly. "You're staying at Africa House?"
She nodded. "I'll take you back then. There's nothing
else to do."

She felt weak with relief because bellowing thunder
warned that the storm was fast approaching. The sky
overhead was a truly threatening black now. Grateful
to Derek, she forgot everything but her own gladness
to be driven someplace safe and warm and dry before
the sky opened up with its deluge. "Thank you!" she
whispered, then on an impulse even she didn't un-

derstand she reached out and laid her hand across his forearm.

At once, however, he pulled away. He glanced at her with a wary, calculating expression. "Get in!" he nodded toward his own jeep with an abrupt toss of his head. Shocked at the transformation of his expression, Cathy stared. She stood unmoving for a second because she really didn't understand his reaction. And because she hesitated, he gestured with a fresh burst of angry impatience.

"I said, get in!"

chapter 2

DEREK HADN'T EVEN started the engine before rain began to fall on the jeep in a steady stream, pinging its metal roof like thousands of hard, dangerous steel pellets.

"This storm is going to be a bad one," Derek said. "It's coming on too fast and too hard for this time of year." With a swift, decisive movement then, he started the car.

Cathy folded her arms protectively over her chest and stared out at the storm gathering momentum beyond the windshield. Already washed clean by the sudden downpour, the glass sparkled beneath the

19

rhythmic movement of the wipers. Through the wind-driven rain beyond she could see clearly her uncle's Land-Rover. She glanced at Derek and felt a sudden renewal of gratitude.

"I hate to think what might have happened if you hadn't come along," she admitted candidly. "No matter what is between us, I do thank you for this ride. I honestly appreciate your help."

"I know," he replied curtly. But then he smiled warmly, letting her know she didn't have to explain her confused feelings.

The unexpected tenderness in his expression, the understanding he communicated, pierced her heart. She felt a stab of poignant loss. They could never be friends, she knew; too much had existed between them. Or could they? The question inspired a burst of dissatisfaction that soured her insides. A thought she hadn't invited sprang to mind. She would taste his mouth on her own once more, she would savor his lean hard weight as he took her in his arms . . . or else become a stranger to him so that they wouldn't have to come in close contact again. It was, clearly, an "either-or" situation for her.

Aching from a clash of unwelcome emotions, Cathy turned away, staring out of the window. The turmoil of the storm whipping the surrounding land into chaos mirrored the storm in her own heart. They rode for miles in silence, enduring a tense, uncomfortable kind of quiet that kept her nerves jangling. From time to time she dared to steal a glance at him, then tore her gaze hastily away because somehow their eyes always met.

Finally, perhaps because he, too, could no longer stand the tension, he spoke. "You haven't been back long, have you? I think I would have known if you were here." Suddenly he frowned. "But then again maybe not. Your uncle tends to keep pretty much to himself just as I do. I haven't associated with the neighbors in the last few months since I came back. Haven't done any more socializing than when I lived here six years ago." He sounded bitter.

"Uncle Howard is very ill," Cathy said softly. "I suppose that has something to do with the news of my arrival not reaching you."

"Howard, ill?" Derek seemed surprised.

"Yes, unfortunately. That's why I'm here." She explained how she had returned at her uncle's request to help him run the preserve. She thought of the work there was to do: monitoring the herds and prides for signs of disease or trouble; supervising the tribesmen hired to patrol the borders of the estate as watchmen. There were people who were curious and people who were mischief makers and none of them seemed to recognize the seriousness of some of their intrusions into the lives of the animals. And worse—there were the game hunters who killed beautiful beasts, not for food, but for the so-called "sport" of it.

"And so he sent for you." Derek sounded almost as though he were speaking to himself. He looked at Cathy, one eyebrow cocked sarcastically. "And what on earth did he think *you* could accomplish? Why, you can't even drive one of his cars without wrecking it!"

"Not everything to do with running a preserve centers around mechanical skill! As a matter of fact, not much of my work has a single thing to do with engines and oil." Her hands balled into fists. She glared defiantly at him.

Deathly tired of hearing him harp about what she did to her uncle's car, Cathy whipped around to glare at him. "You act like it's *your* Land-Rover I burned up," she cried. "You talk as if you're the one who'll have to deal with it!"

With eyes straight ahead as he speeded along the still blessedly firm road, Derek's jaw appeared cast in some unyielding metal and his teeth were clenched as he spoke. "You're right. It's none of my business, and thank goodness for it. But if you had been a little less careless, I might have been spared the inconvenience of bringing you back to your uncle."

"Well, don't do me any favors!" she cried.

Something snapped deep inside her and mindlessly she reached for the door handle. She had already started to yank the door open when he, seeing that she was about to fling herself from the car still traveling at a good thirty miles an hour, screeched to a halt. He grabbed her.

"Idiot!" His strong arms hauled her roughly across the seat and close to his side. "You crazy little fool! Are you trying to kill yourself?"

His arms pressed tight around her, imprisoning her, and the force of his angry embrace hurt her. Catching his breath, he held her so close against him that she could feel his heart pounding.

In the crisis of the moment his hand had fallen accidentally against her breast, and lingered there palm down. He held her quivering against him. The sensation of his intimate touch caused a tingle to ripple from the middle of her chest up her throat. Her breasts went taut; her flesh heated in sudden wild excitement.

Unwilling to move or even to breathe, both remained silent. His warmth surrounded her. His body pressed against her from behind. Frozen where he held her, Cathy listened to his breathing. Its normal rhythm had intensified, lashed into hungry eagerness not only from the sensation of her soft skin pressed against his, but also from the knowledge that his touch had so aroused her, she was sure. No doubt he could hear her arousal in the trembling way she inhaled. He could feel it under his palm against her breast. Oh, yes, her body had betrayed the feelings that pride would fight to hide.

For a breathless eternity his hand remained, neither pulling free nor pressing tighter to take liberties, yet from every sign his body also unwillingly revealed, she knew how badly he desired her too. Giddy from this unexpectedly exciting force, she reached shyly for his hand. Six years seemed to have melted away.

"Derek," she whispered in a voice trembling with yearning and invitation.

At once she regretted her boldness... bitterly regretted it. He reacted to the touch of her fingers as if a live electrical wire had sent its shock burning through him. He broke away. With a swift move he locked her door, then drew back into his own seat, a grim expression on his face.

"D-Derek?"

"Your uncle will be wondering about you." His voice was low and savage. He yanked the car back into gear and with a jolt roared forward again, quickly reaching an alarming speed as he jammed his foot harder and harder on the accelerator. He rammed the jeep through ever deepening mud. With an abrupt gesture he thrust a cassette into his tape deck. Its stormy classical roar matched not only the weather outside but obviously his own mood as well.

"You...you seem to have done rather well for yourself," she said nervously.

"What of it?" he snapped back. "I had nothing better to do with my time than to succeed. Certainly I had no woman to divert my energy."

"How fortunate for you!" she commented sardonically.

As the pitch of the music rose, he turned to her. Cathy recoiled under his burning gaze which pinned her to the door she leaned against and held her like a butterfly imprisoned on a panel of velvet. His eyes glittered with mockery.

Because he had rejected her own eager need with contempt, Cathy was filled with an angry emotion close to hate. She glared at him, then looked away, holding her head high as she gazed unseeing out the front window. She became aware of the speed of the jeep and wanted to screw her eyes shut and cower. Derek was driving like a maniac, flinging great puddles of mud and water up from the wheels, taking the road like a victory-maddened conqueror intent upon rape and pillage. Cathy glanced at him, alarmed now by the wildness of his mood dictating the way he handled the jeep. Suddenly up ahead, too close on the slippery road, she saw a file of zebras fleeing from the storm to shelter.

"Derek, watch out!" she cried, while he, eyes widened, muttered something under his breath. With brakes screeching and face grim, he yanked the steering wheel hard to the left to avoid the animals. Cathy screamed as the jeep spun around, whirling now like a maddened dancer in the slippery mud. Staring through the windshield, her eyes widened. They had come to the edge of a horribly deep ditch. The jeep's front wheels passed over it and then the rear did too as they hurtled off solid ground.

chapter 3

THE JEEP JOLTED down the steep incline into the ditch. Every muscle in Derek's arms strained as he wrenched the wheel. His lips curled back from gritted teeth and his eyes squinted tight in concentration as he struggled to keep the jeep under some semblance of control. He braked sharply and came to a violent halt.

Cathy shot forward, flinging out both arms, fully expecting them to be broken. But instead of the bone-grinding, skin-bruising contact of metal against her body, she met a sudden softness that made her gasp in yet another moment of shocked surprise. Yards of air-filled plastic had swelled out from beneath the dashboard to cushion her and Derek. She shuddered, then gulped air to steady her quivering nerves, able to think only of how impressed and grateful she was that Derek had been clever enough to equip his jeep with air bags.

At last Derek's voice came through the thick silence. "Are you all right, Cathy?" He sounded genuinely worried about her.

"I . . . I think so." She laughed shakily. "Lucky for us your car comes equipped with instant padding."

Derek yanked the door open, jumped out, and ran around to pull her free from the mess cluttering the front seats and dashboard. As he helped her to a standing position, his hands lingered on her back. Instinctively she stepped into his embrace. They didn't move, wrapped in one another's arms, the rain pouring down on them as they slowly overcame the impact of the accident. The thunder still boomed, but ever louder, warning that the heaviest of the storm approached. It was that great, ominous sound which forced them apart. Both knew they had to find shelter . . . and fast.

Cathy shuddered. Africa House was miles away. Could she and Derek find a farmhouse, a native village, someplace where they'd be taken in? She dreaded thinking about the cold, wet, and nasty night they'd spend otherwise. "What will we do?" she asked softly.

Derek was quiet, thoughtful for a moment. "I have a small lodge not too far from here," he said. "I use it when I want to get off by myself. Best of all it has a fireplace." He paused and again Cathy sensed his reluctance. "We can stay there 'til the rain stops . . . or at least slows."

"But what about my uncle? He'll be incredibly worried."

"Can't be notified. I don't have a phone, so just forget it. You don't think there's any way I can get you to him now?" He tossed his proud white-blond mane of hair in the direction of his jeep, the all too familiar mocking glitter lighting his eyes. "You're a damned jinx, Cathy. Two accidents with you! And you wrecked your uncle's jeep. I swear no one should ever be in or near a car you've even seen, much less touched!"

She glared at him with little effect. If anything, he appeared amused... infuriatingly so.

"Let's get going," she mumbled angrily, then whirled around to start marching away. But the effect was quite lost when she stumbled on a rock buried in the mud and very nearly fell. Derek steadied her, holding her against him as they struggled up the slight incline. His hand scarcely left the small of her back as he guided her to his lodge.

When she finally glimpsed the structure Derek indicated was their destination, her eyes widened. Her impression was confirmed: he had done very well indeed. Half-hidden by a stand of trees, the modern, sweeping lines of the building were so pleasing that Cathy was sure the architect was a sensitive artist. He had captured the mood of the setting and reflected the natural beauties in his design. Wood, brick, great stretches of glass—an impressive "lodge," as Derek had called it, and an ever so welcome one, too.

"Thank heavens!" Cathy exclaimed. She dashed for

the wide doorway, Derek at her heels. Rivulets of water trickled off her body into a pool around her feet.

He pulled a key from his pocket. "I know I probably don't need to secure this door," he said, following her in, "but it is a habit I picked up in Johannesburg."

"Johannesburg? What were you doing in Johannesburg?"

Derek shrugged. "Making my fortune. In mining."

So that was it—diamonds or gold, or one of South Africa's other mineral resources had proven lucky for him. "South Africa was good to you. Far better than here. It's a wonder you came back at all...even for a visit." She did not bother to hide her acid tone of voice.

"Malawi is my home—and you know it! I merely lived in Johannesburg long enough to accomplish what I had set out to do."

She chilled at the brooding hardness she saw in his eyes. Something about the way they glinted like blue-tinted ice as he looked back at her stifled the questions she wanted to ask. She glanced around and tried to change the subject.

"This...this is really a nice place. From what you said, I had expected something else, more a humble log cabin in these woods."

Derek merely snorted, and Cathy wandered away, unashamedly inspecting the place. It matched in its own way the lean, hard simplicity of Derek's body...and character. Planks of blond-reddish wood covered the walls and were hung with African art—masks and carvings from all over the continent. Plump, modular furniture, upholstered in black corduroy, was dramatic, yet practical. The rich-looking pieces could form arrangements suiting his moods and needs at a given moment. Two wooden tables stood waiting within easy reach of the couch to hold drinks or plates of food.

In the center of this great circular room stood the fireplace to which he'd referred earlier. Actually it was an open wood stove of Swedish modern design, vented by a pipe through the cone-shaped ceiling. Though still unlit, its very presence welcomed them. It invited the two chilled, wet wayfarers to fill it with logs and kindling and to light the fire that would warm them. When Cathy saw it, she became aware again of how her clothes clung to her skin, how the gooseflesh rose. She was shivering and her teeth began to chatter.

Derek noticed her discomfort. His rugged face softened with sympathy. "I'm sorry. I'll get right on this." He knelt and began to build the fire carefully, then lit it with an extra-long match. As the fire caught, flames licking high, Cathy moved close to it, stretching her bluish fingers toward the crackling warmth. People back in the States always seemed to think of Africa as one sprawling continent with a supremely hot, tropical climate. Most forgot—or never knew—how many different African countries there are each with its own vegetation, wildlife, climate. And the climate here in the Shire River Valley was temperate, mild. Still, even with the thermostat registering in the sixty degree range the breeze-driven dampness could penetrate and chill one's bones, and so a fireplace was a delightful, extraordinarily comforting luxury.

Derek brought her a blanket. "Here, take off those wet things and wrap yourself in this."

Cathy glanced at it, then raised her large green eyes to Derek.

"Is there any place I can go to change, or do you expect me to perform a striptease for you as payment for my room and board?" She spoke sharply to hide her discomfort.

He was not amused by her sarcastic offer, but answered coldly. "You'll find the bathroom through the door." He nodded toward a break in the paneling, a door she hadn't noticed in her earlier, swift appraisal of the large room.

Cathy flushed but said nothing. Huffing a little, she turned and with her chin pushed high stood to leave. As she moved past, however, walking on the thick chocolate-brown pile carpet, his low, throaty chuckle followed after. Sensing that Derek was mocking her, she whipped around to glare at him, then stopped short. His eyes held her own with a knowing glitter.

Cathy whirled, then ran from the room, anxious to reach the sterile, fluorescent-lit privacy of his bathroom. What right had he to be so overbearing? No matter how lucky he had been in Johannesburg, he was still the same Derek Guenther she had known as a ragged outcast youth here in Malawi. Nothing could change that. Though the rest of the world saw him as he had become, she would always think of him as he was, and what he had done to hurt her. Cathy's cheeks burned with outrage.

She peeled off her sodden halter top and unsnapped her wet and clinging shorts. When she'd managed to wiggle free of them, she briskly toweled her body, turning the pale gooseflesh into rosy, warm skin. She draped the blanket over her shoulders, and chuckled aloud at a wicked impulse that suddenly tempted her. Derek had walked away once, proving his soul-deep indifference. She would make him regret it!

So he despised her as a person, she thought, but he hardly despised her body. Her green eyes narrowed catlike as she calculated her next move. "We'll see just how aloof our dear Derek Guenther can be!" she whispered to herself.

A voice deep inside, undoubtedly her better judgment, warned that she was playing with fire. The way he had pushed away from her with angry, brutal harshness still rankled. She should have been the one to reject when, after all, it was she who had been wronged. Cathy's full, soft lips curved into a smile, but her emerald eyes glittered with determination.

Derek would bite for the bait she was about to hold out for him. When he did, Cathy intended giving him a taste of his very own medicine. She looked into the mirror. She was tiny, a scant three inches over five feet tall, small-boned and slender. In womanly curves, however, nature had blessed her well, even though annoyingly early. Her high breasts curved full and firm. Below her tiny waist were well-rounded hips. Her skin glowed with almost translucent ivory perfection.

Her long-lashed eyes seemed brilliantly green in the

room's fluorescent glare. A bloom of reddish pink lingered on her cheeks. Looking at herself as if studying a stranger in the mirror, Cathy smiled, pleased by what she saw. As a child she had needed braces. Going into adolescence she had cursed the mouthful of hardware inflicted on her by the orthodontist and her conscientious parents. Now, every day when she caught her smile in a mirror, she blessed them. Her teeth were perfectly straight and gleamed like mother-of-pearl.

Being neither blind nor stupid, Cathy knew why men had always found her desirable. She had dated seriously first one, then a second, thoroughly nice man during the past few years. Both had been devoted to her. And, despite her warm feelings for them, attraction even, a deep reservation, an obstinate, bullheaded pride kept her from giving to either what she had lavished on Derek. Because Derek Guenther had rejected what others had wanted, and sometimes wanted desperately, Cathy vowed that she'd make him want her most of all. Then she'd let him burn!

She yanked her long black hair free from its braids to hang wet and wavy down her back. In an hour or so it would dry, becoming soft, lush, thick, hanging past her shoulders almost to her waist. She had no lipstick, so she bit her lips hard until they were rosy. She glanced with satisfaction at the blanket and its color—a rich deep plum hue. With her blue-black hair, green eyes, and ivory skin, the color was most becoming.

Instead of huddling inside the blanket, she wrapped it around her body, tossing an end over one shoulder in a fair imitation of a graceful sari. To her delight she found in the medicine cabinet a bottle of very expensive French perfume. Cathy smiled as she pulled the stopper, then daubed a fair amount on her wrists, earlobes, inner elbows, and between her breasts in the spot where she soon hoped to lure Derek Guenther into the first step of his decline and fall.

"Hey, you all right in there?" he called to her from the other side of the door.

"Just fine," she answered. She smiled one last time at the mirror, then turned, determined to begin to get her revenge. Feeling confident now that she could conquer even this impossible man, Cathy opened the door, pushed it wide, then stepped out into the room with a seductive smile on her face.

She saw at once that her efforts had their effect. Derek's eyes widened. His lips parted. A half-inhaled breath caught somewhere between his throat and chest and remained suspended for an instant until he finally remembered to let it out again in a low but audible sigh. He stood without speaking, pulsing with emotion, his eyes running up and down her body. She, waiting in a promisingly yielding posture, knew his seduction would prove easy. Without warning, though, his eyes narrowed.

"D-Derek?" she whispered. She felt suddenly uncertain. Anger wasn't in her plan, only desire—aroused at her choosing. "What—what is it? What's wrong?"

"You're terribly transparent, my dear."

She recoiled to see how his expression flared to a

fire that had nothing to do with lust. She flushed, but resolved she would carry this through to the end, no matter where it led her. "I-I don't know what you mean."

"Oh, don't you?" His voice crooned low and menacing. "You come out with your hair down and that blanket exposing as much as it's covering, and you expect that I'll be so stupid that I don't know what you're up to? Especially since I happen to share your sentiments in reverse."

"What *am* I up to then?" Cathy raised her eyes, challenging him. His response was not what she expected.

He pushed away from the wall against which he was leaning. His gaze burned into her as he came closer to where she stood.

Horrified, trying not to cower visibly, her lashes fluttered as she blinked on a sudden spasm of fear. She began to remember the warning from deeper inside herself and regretted that she had chosen to ignore it.

His eyes were pinned to her face. He focused there as if he dared not glance lower to the inviting curve of her breasts with their white swells visible above the rough plum-colored wool. He kept his eyes fixed well away from her hips, full and womanly. Still, the hot, luminous intensity of his eyes frightened her as he approached, until, drawing up, he hovered over her— taller than she by many inches and strong with muscles lean and hard from a life of vigorous exercise.

No matter what was to come, no matter what the cost in pain or struggle, Cathy knew she would not let Derek Guenther feel he had defeated her. She must somehow turn whatever happened into her own victory of pride. She drew herself as tall as she could and stared at him defiantly. "Since you seem so sure of your ability to read my mind, *you* tell *me*! What *am* I up to?"

His eyes narrowed, their color deepening into a dark, threatening hue the color of stormy skies. She held her ground, meeting his gaze unflinchingly. It had seemed unthinkable that he might try to force her, but now she realized she couldn't be sure.

She would fight if he did, of course, and suffer badly for her foolishness. Even that, however, could be turned against him in one way or the other. Standing terrified in front of him now, but trying not to show it, Cathy vowed she'd make him suffer somehow if he dared.

His eyes never left her face. For that one endless second the silence between them felt thick enough to choke on. Finally he answered her. "Do you want me to tell you or show you?" His voice gritted deadly soft from behind his teeth. Though barely audible, it vibrated with rage held in check.

Not daring to move, Cathy stood in his shadow and returned the look in his eyes with a proud challenge of her own. "I really wonder that *you* could show me anything." She tossed her head. She had been about to make some snide remark about the bottle of perfume in his bathroom and use it somehow to put down his masculinity. Suddenly, however, he grabbed her wrist.

"You asked for it, little one!" he snapped. His eyes

sizzled. His face paled beneath his tan.

Cathy recoiled. "Derek!" she whispered, then cried out as he yanked her roughly to his body. Holding her tight, he smashed a hard angry kiss upon her lips.

His arms were like steel clamps pinning her, making her utterly helpless. Even through the thick wool of her makeshift sari, she felt his passion raging through him. She jerked her head back in a movement that surprised Derek so he released her lips and ever so slightly his hold on her.

"No, please!" she whispered. Her eyes had grown very large and imploring. She tried to writhe free, but her desperation was no match for his strength.

Sure that the very worst was about to happen, Cathy tried to kick at him. She reached up to claw his face and even to bite, but with no luck. Ignoring her efforts, overpowering them all by angry force, Derek swept her off her feet and carried her to a low flat arrangement of hassocks that together formed a space about the size of a double bed.

"Derek, no!" Sobbing aloud in terror, Cathy pounded against his back with her fists.

Like a Tartar at rampage he flung her down. She tried to squirm away, but he was on top of her too fast, his weight crushing her.

He kissed her, his lips brutal on her mouth. And then, suddenly, he grew gentle. A delicious shiver rippled through her as his mouth explored the tender flesh of her neck. His lips savored the skin below her ear then dropped lower to whisper little kisses against the hollow of her throat. The blanket had come un-

wrapped. His palms touched bare skin. His hands
moved on her shoulders, dropped to explore and tenderly possess the soft, womanly richness of her breasts.
Under his knowing caress, her breasts grew taut. Trembling with aroused hunger, Cathy inhaled deep, shuddering breaths. His touch had awakened once again
all her yearning, unfilled need. And tear-glazed eyes
pleaded for him to do as he had done before, six
summers earlier.

As he pulled his hand away to stroke her hair flowing thick and silken down her back, she ached for him
to hold her hard against him. She lay moaning, white
heat burning through her. "Oh, Derek!" she whispered.
"It's been too long, too long." Forgotten was all her
earlier pain and bitterness.

Lying beneath him, she yearned for him to fondle
the moist perfume-scented place between her breasts.
Her back arched. Desperate for his passion, aching for
him to possess her, she wrapped her arms around his
neck, murmuring his name over and over.

Suddenly, with a fierce cry, he tore himself away
from her. Lying there with eyes wide open, disbelieving, full of wild need, she felt like shouting for
him to come back. She was willing to forgive this
strange and hostile impulse that had come over him,
if only he would sweep her back up immediately into
his arms. "Derek?" she pleaded, reaching out to him.

"You'd like that, wouldn't you?" He bit off each
word with savage intensity. "This wasn't in your little
plan, was it? *You* were supposed to be the one to do
the seducing and the pushing away, weren't you?"

His eyes ravaged her as she lay naked under his gaze. She pulled at the blanket to cover herself and protect the few shreds that remained of her pride. Throbbing with humiliation, she stared at him, unable to believe he had rejected her just when she would have given him the sweet, yielding hunger of her womanhood.

His scorn was withering. She drew herself into a sitting position. Desire had not yet subsided from her flesh, but remained aching in its futility. Her lips, struggling to part and shout some insult at him, trembled from the intensity of her shame and rage. She felt the sobs rising from deep inside, but choked them back.

"Hurt your pride?" He stood over her, arms folded across his chest, and gazed down at her with grim satisfaction. "Turn about's fair play, Cathy!"

"Go to the devil!" She whipped her head away, cursing herself for having yielded to him. She damned herself for crying out his name. Now when it was all over, she loathed herself for the tears she barely held back. Why hadn't she learned her lesson first time around?

"Righteous indignation does not become you," he said, watching her.

"You're a swine!" She lashed out at him. "You always were!"

"Out of your league, aren't you?" Again, it was not really a question, but a statement of fact spoken with infuriating smugness. "It'll teach you not to play with fire, little one."

"So what have you proved?" she cried, glaring at him. "Does it make you feel any more of a man? You've about as much heart as a stone carving. I see now you haven't changed a bit, not since you walked away from that accident leaving *me* to be dragged out by strangers."

"Cathy—!" Derek stared, stunned. "That's not how it was at all, and you know it!"

"I know what I know!" She forced herself to speak with deadly intensity, though her entire body trembled. "Why didn't you come to see me in the hospital, Derek? Why did you dump me? Considering what we had done—what we had shared—you could have visited at least once!"

"What the hell are you talking about?" he demanded angrily. "*You* were the one who gave *me* the brushoff, you and your whole damned household."

Cathy's eyes blazed. "You're crazy, Derek!" she cried. "Either that or you're lying through your teeth. I already knew you were a swine, but are you a liar, too?"

Suddenly what she had dreaded began to happen. Her body shuddered with great, wracking sobs that came so fast she could hardly breathe.

Derek sat down quickly beside her, taking her in his arms. He tried to hold her close, to stroke her head as if comforting a child, but she fought away, resisting him. "Let me go, damn you!" she cried, fists pounding against him. Her voice was shrill, tears blinded her eyes.

"Cathy, for God's sake, listen to me!" Though she

struggled hard against him, he would not let her go, but if anything, held her closer.

"Cathy, I didn't know what happened. No one would tell me anything—certainly not where you were—only that you had gone away and wanted nothing further to do with me."

"Of course, of course!" she shouted. "What kind of intelligence does it take to figure out I'd be in a hospital? There aren't that many hospitals around here . . . and for *that* matter, why'd you run off the way you did, Derek? Why did you leave me there for someone else to find?" Anger dried her tears. She turned her head, unable to bear the sight of him any longer. She loathed herself, too, for having wanted him so badly even after all he had done to hurt her.

"Cathy, I didn't know. I didn't."

"What are you talking about?" she lashed at him scornfully. "You had eyes. You could have seen I was unconscious."

"Damn it, Cathy!" he bellowed. "I was unconscious too . . . in a way. I must have wandered some, though I don't remember any of it, because I woke up in a native village with a hell of a bad headache and no idea how many days I'd been there. And my rescuers couldn't help. You know Nyanja tribesmen don't keep track of time, at least not the way we do."

"Oh, Derek!" She could hardly choke out his name. "I wish I could believe you . . . I wish I could, but I can't!"

He let out a long angry snort and it rekindled Cathy's own anger. His story sounded too easy, too convenient. Did he expect that this single glib explanation could be believed? And if so that it could erase all the hurt? He knew how difficult it would be to disprove him. After all, six years had gone by. Who would remember? Who would know?

Once recovered, he could have asked around. This was such a small place and everyone knew everyone else's business. Someone would have told him she was still in Malawi, in the hospital. She had lain there for a long time recovering. He could have called and a phone clerk would have told him her room number. Nothing could have stopped him—if he really had cared. Cathy frowned. She was so confused.

"Leave me alone, Derek!" She turned her head and then lay down, curling her body. She shivered, not so much from chill as emotion, and drew her knees up to her chest, rocking a little for comfort.

Derek paced, his steps muted by the thick carpet. The rain struck the roof and windows with numbing rhythm. She was exhausted emotionally and physically and soon began to drift into sleep. She felt Derek tuck the blanket securely around her and then move quietly away.

Through only the tiniest crack between her lashes, she watched him as he walked over to the fireplace and put another log on the fire. With a pang of uncertainty she wondered about him. Was he telling the truth? Right then, however, overwhelmed by weariness, she couldn't deal with such questioning. She slept, but not really restfully because angry, troubled dreams bedeviled her until morning.

chapter 4

CHILLY GRAY DAWN crept in while Cathy slept, bringing with it a sharp noise as the rain, still pounding hard, beat a brisk rhythm against the windowpanes. The sound penetrated her dream, bringing her slowly awake.

The rough wool blanket was heavy upon her. The bristling fibers of its yarn prickled her naked skin. Memory welled of how she had craved Derek, and she grimaced in shame. A fire crackled in the hearth. The way it glowed, alive and strong from logs newly fed to it, told her Derek was already up and around. She sat up. Her eyes swept past the empty living room to his small, efficient kitchen. To her surprise she saw no sign of him in the cold morning light. At once her heart plummeted with an odd combination of relief and dismay. Where was he? Why had he left her here all alone? She dreaded seeing him again, yet at the same time looked forward to it with hopeful, yearning eagerness.

Clouds as dark as her mood choked out the sun. A wind had come up. It rattled the windows and whistled around the corners of the rustic, yet luxurious lodge. Derek's hideaway, she thought, trying to be scornful. But she was impressed. The house had been designed in an open, free and airy style. Essentially it was one huge room. Other than the bathroom, no fixed walls divided the interior space into separate rooms. Only a chest-high bar marked the boundaries of the kitchen. Had Derek been anywhere inside, she would have seen him. She knew she ought to be thankful, at least, that Derek had stoked and fed the fire so she would be cozy. There was nothing quite so cheerful on a gloomy day as a brightly burning fire. It couldn't, however, really diminish either her growing apprehension or her irrational resentment at finding herself abandoned.

It was a good thing she'd be going back to Africa House soon. Once safely away, she'd never have to lay eyes on Derek again. No doubt he would be just as glad to be rid of her. She smiled a little ruefully at the thought. For Derek, too, this encounter must be difficult—to say the least.

Cathy rose quickly. Her clothes, wrinkled but dry, lay on a chair near the fire. She scrambled into the brief outfit and twirled the blanket around her for warmth. She wandered to one of the windows, peered out, and frowned, impatient and uneasy. Enough was enough! She wanted to get home. Uncle Howard was probably worried to death. The Franklins, too. The older couple, about her uncle's own age, was hired by him years ago as caretakers and general assistants, had come to be far more than mere employees of Tanyasi. To Uncle Howard they were good and loyal friends; to Cathy they were the grandparents she had never known.

Now that daylight had come, Derek would find some way of getting her back home, some other transportation to replace the jeep that went into the ditch. He *had* to. No way would she—*could* she—stay here with him. Even if Uncle Howard hadn't been a consideration, too much still remained between herself and Derek. She had never recovered from the hurt and pain his disappearance had inflicted, and no amount of explaining could make her forget what she had been through. Even though he had spoken with such sincerity last night about his reasons, she could not believe him.

He had known her uncle disapproved of him, so why had he accepted without question the story that she didn't want him near her again? Even if he were telling the truth, he should have known better. Lord knows, he had plenty of time to make inquiries and learn where they had taken her. She had lain in traction in that miserable room for a month—far longer than it would have taken for his head injury to heal. She couldn't visualize the rebellious, passionate youth Derek had been holding back. It just wasn't like him. In fact, the more she thought about his explanation, the more flimsy it became. He had stayed away by choice that summer long ago. He had abandoned her. And on that bitterly painful decision, she reassured herself with fierce intensity that the passion he had aroused in her last night was cold, finished, gone forever.

She heard the sloshing of rubber boots over the sounds of the storm as the one wearing them slowly approached the cedar-stained back door. Through the window carved into its upper half she saw a yellow oilcloth cap pulled low. Its brim touched the upturned collar of a matching raincoat. Both effectively concealed the face underneath.

Cathy warily watched the figure who reached out to open the door. As his hand gripped the knob, she tensed, then relaxed. It was Derek, of course, who pushed open the door. His raincoat, hat, and galoshes dripped, forming puddles on the brown-tiled kitchen floor. With a sigh, he pulled off his hat, then flung it down on the table.

"Where did you go?" she demanded. Uneasiness put a harsh edge on her voice.

"Out . . . to see how things are." His tension matched hers.

"What about your jeep?"

"What about it?"

"Well, didn't you *do* anything?"

Derek shrugged. "What *can* I do? The gully's

flooded and the storm is getting worse. Even if I pulled it out, which I can't do right now, it wouldn't run. And the way things are going, it seems the whole damned river is about to overspill its banks."

"Well, how am I supposed to get home without the car?" Her voice was sharp, shrill.

"That's the very *least* of our worries," he replied in a grim tone. "In any case, I'm afraid you can't."

"What? What do you mean, I can't?"

"Just what I said. When the weather calms down, I'll think of a way but—"

"Calms down?" she cried out in an exasperated voice. "There can be rain for *days*!" She had lived in Malawi before. She *knew*.

"Then we'll just have to be brave and wait it out." His voice revealed sardonic amusement. His smirk infuriated her.

Cathy's eyes widened, flashing fire as she glared at him. "We can't!" she gasped. The very idea of spending any more time with him horrified her. She couldn't bear it. "If you think I'm going to stay here any longer . . . any longer than *today*, well, you're sadly mistaken."

Derek stood with arms folded across his chest.

"As far as I can see, neither one of us is going *anywhere*."

"That's what *you* think!" Cathy stomped toward the door, snatching the hat he'd left on the table. Under no circumstances would she spend days, or even hours, alone with Derek Guenther. Not anymore. Not after last night.

She grabbed a raincoat from a peg by the door. Hand on the knob, she tossed one final defiant look at Derek. She flung open the door but before she could even step over the threshold, he stopped her.

Kicking the door shut, he pushed her back into the room. He wasn't angry. More alarming than that, he seemed tender.

"Oh, Cathy," he reached out and grasped her hand. "God, you're a beautiful fool! Seeing you again..." He went on, strangely breathless, barely whispering the words. "I never forgot you, never stopped wanting you. Never!"

Her green eyes were wide; her mouth was parted in surprise.

"Oh, I tried," he went on. "I lied to myself, but deep down I always knew." His sigh came out half aloud in a moan. He lifted her hand and kissed each finger slowly, eyes intent on her all the while. Then he pulled her abruptly into a tight embrace. "I was a fool not to finish what you started last night, a damn pigheaded fool." He whispered into her ear. "You were so ripe, so willing, and I wanted you. Lord, how I wanted you!" He nibbled her earlobe and his intention was obvious. Now. He would do now what he wanted to do last night.

Even if Cathy were willing to believe what he had told her of his disappearance those years ago, she could not so easily forget how he had rejected her last night. She could not ignore her hurt pride, or the hungry, unsatisfied aching.

To brace herself and clear her head, she gulped in

a deep breath. He caressed her so tenderly. Resisting
him with everything inside her, she stiffened her muscles. She pushed away so he could see her face. Her
eyes were wide, frozen open as she glared at him.
"Get your hands off me, Derek Guenther!"

His response was to kiss her angry mouth. Then,
the very hands she had demanded to take away, softened their grip and slid downward, palms flat, in a
sweet, slow caress that nearly melted away her cold
resolve. "Cathy!" he murmured huskily.

She was responding, heart pounding, excitement
mounting. Suddenly with a burst of shame for her own
weakness she remembered herself—who she was and
why she had such good reason to resist Derek. Flushing
angrily, she pushed away again, writhing to break free.

"You had your chance, Derek," she cried. "Last
night proved how little you really care about me. You
were the one to turn away, and I can't forgive you.
And now, this morning, you suddenly want to do what
you wouldn't do last night. You expect me just to go
meekly along. Well, forget it!"

"Damn it, Cathy!" He stared at her in angry frus-
tration but did not try to stop her. She glared at him
in defiance as she backed out of his reach, then just
stood facing him, challenging him to come closer.
What lasting joy could she hope to find in the arms
of this man whose passion only aroused bitter memories? They stared hard at one another, mesmerized
by emotion.

"What now?" she asked after a long time when her
anger had subsided into cold, despairing resignation.

He shrugged, apparently as unhappy as she. "Make the best of our enforced stay together, I guess." He paused. "Are you hungry? You could eat breakfast."

Suddenly Cathy realized she *was* hungry. She had forgotten all about food yesterday afternoon and evening. At the mere mention of it now, she felt pangs stabbing her stomach. She remembered with a shock that almost twenty-four hours had passed since she had eaten. "Yes, breakfast!" she said. "I take it you have some food stashed away here somewhere."

"You'll find it all in those cupboards over there." He indicated cabinets hung on the kitchen's far wall. "Fix whatever you like for us."

For some reason that had nothing to do with common sense or logic, his flat tone stung. "Fix it yourself!"

Derek raised his eyebrows but said nothing as he turned and walked away. "You're the one who's hungry," he observed. "Frankly it's not food *I* crave."

She threw him a dirty look and flounced into the kitchen, flinging open the pantry cupboards and searching in them, making an angry clatter.

There was little on the shelves. It was obvious Derek hadn't used the lodge for some time or else his habit was to bring fresh food when he came. His refrigerator stood dark and empty. She looked at the shelves again. She could choose between sardines packed in tomato sauce, canned beef stew, or assorted tinned vegetables and fruits. A miserable selection. With a sigh she reached for the beef stew. It seemed the least offensive choice for breakfast.

As she heated it in a pan, she glanced at Derek from time to time. Good Lord, the way she'd been behaving with him! All passion and wild emotion. Her warm, understanding heart and her cool, logical brain seemed lost in his presence. Perhaps it was the surprise of their meeting on the road with her in such a foolish fix and him as the rescuer, then all the subsequent bizarre events. Whatever, she knew she'd been acting just like the overly emotional, slightly rebellious girl she'd been before. It was frightening—this spiraling back in time, losing the hard-won independence and maturity of the last six years. Where was the woman who'd willingly come here to help her uncle? Was the adult Cathy merely lost for a few hours to the physically overdeveloped child who responded to Derek without reason or balance?

She looked down at the stew and frowned in disgust, then quickly removed the pan from the heat so it wouldn't scorch. Her childish behavior had extended even to the matter of food! She took a can of mixed fruits from the shelves, found powdered milk and coffee. She wrinkled her nose. These items wouldn't make much of a meal, but certainly something a little better, a little more civilized than a can of stew slopped into a bowl and put on a bare table. While the coffee brewed, she set the table.

There was only the sound of rain, broken by an occasional spit of crackling wood in the fireplace. Calming down, beginning to feel and behave more her true self of the recent past, Cathy felt almost normal again—even somewhat at peace. But then she looked across the room at Derek and her nerves tightened.

Derek stared out the window. A deep frown creased his high forehead and he seemed curiously intent, poised almost. She followed his gaze and suddenly recalled the time the Shire River had flooded when she was a child. It had been an awesome event in her young life. Her eyes darted back to Derek and then again to the window, holding on the view of the steady downpour. Just how many hours had it been raining this *hard*? Too many! She glanced at Derek again... and knew there was danger from the storm for them. If her memory and sense hadn't said so, Derek's tense posture would have. She took a deep breath. Grace under pressure... that was courage. And she tried for a moment in vain to recall where she'd read or heard that definition.

"Breakfast," she sang out on a note of decidedly false cheer that made her add quickly, "such as it is."

Derek turned in swift surprise, eyes quickly appraising Cathy, then the table she'd set. His eyebrows rose a fraction before he started toward her. She quickly served the sketchy meal and accepted Derek's help in seating her. He leaned over her shoulder after he'd pushed in the chair.

"A truce, I gather. Or is it still war and you've poisoned my food?"

Cathy's mouth curved in a soft smile at the light charm of his voice. "I've never been the devious type. Have no fear."

He was lowering himself into the chair opposite her. "Never?" he asked with pointed mockery.

Cathy's breath caught at his meaning. She'd intended to be *quite* devious the night before and her plan had boomeranged—to say the least! She looked him straight in the eye. "Hardly ever—and never successfully!" It was as much an apology as she could bring herself to make given his more than adequate retribution. "So the food is quite safe, I assure you," she added with a renewed attempt at lightness.

He looked quizzically at her for a moment, then raised his coffee cup in a slight salute before sipping the strong brew well diluted with the powdered milk. "Ah-h, café au lait. That's good," he commented.

Their eyes met, both realizing that by instinct six years after their last meeting, Cathy had prepared Derek's coffee exactly as he liked it.

chapter 5

A POUNDING TATOO sounded at the kitchen door. Startled, Cathy looked up and jerked her head around, seeing in the blur of movement that Derek had leaped up from his seat.

"Oh, thank God!" she gasped. At best, their unexpected visitor would have a jeep or Land-Rover that might get her back to Africa House. At the very least the person out there would be no worse a threat to her peace of mind than Derek, and certainly a defense against the consequences of their continued isolation.

She called out a loud "hello" as Derek flung the door open. She saw a tall, burly stranger who wore a frayed, oil-spotted trench coat that looked old enough to have been left over from the war—World War II! A rubberized rain hat covered his head, its brim folded downward to let the water run off. Hair, variously colored auburn, brown, blond, and gray, tangled together in the beard that bushed from the lower half of his face.

As he moved into the room, she saw how worried his expression was. "We got a little problem upriver," he said to Derek, not bothering with an introduction or any other preliminaries.

"Flooding?" Derek moved toward him now, eyes narrowed and face tensed.

"Aye," the man nodded. "We could use your help, sir, with the sandbagging."

At once Derek nodded, then reached for his coat hanging on the back of a nearby chair. The man continued. "Got two other fellows out back waiting. We can all ride together."

Cathy leaned toward him. "Will you be going anywhere near Africa House?" She stared eagerly, her heart leaping with hope.

"You mean Tanyasi? No, 'fraid not," replied the man shaking his head. By then he had removed his dripping hat. A worried frown seemed permanently furrowed into his brow. "The danger is in the opposite direction, along a bend further north. Africa House— all of Tanyasi—is completely the other way from where we're needed."

Derek turned to Cathy. "Stay here and when the worst is over I'll come back for you."

"Alone? Are you out of your mind?" She looked at him in surprise. Being forced to stay at all was bad enough. She glanced uneasily outdoors. Neither did she care to be stranded, alone without help and little food in such nasty weather.

"Cathy!" Derek's voice took on a grim, warning tone. By the very sound, and the very look of him, she saw he had no intention of allowing her to disobey.

She, however, had other ideas and was in no mood to bow meekly to the will of Derek Guenther, or anyone else for that matter. Just as she opened her mouth to protest, however, the stranger burst in to interrupt.

"The lass is right, mister," he said. "The whole river is swelling and your place lies right in its path should it overflow. She might get flooded out staying here. She'd better come along with us. We can drop her off on the way. She can keep the missus company as she gives her a spot of help, too."

"North of here?" Cathy asked. "If *that's* my choice, I'd rather stay here. I'm trying to get back home, not go further astray."

But Derek had changed his mind at the older man's warning. "Cathy, you're coming with us, so stop wasting time. I'm not going to leave you here if there's danger of the river flooding. That's final." Derek's face hardened.

Cathy stood motionless, staring back with defiance.

"Come along, lass." The stranger spoke gently to her. "It's a hard time for all of us, but you'll be safe upland from here on a bit of a rise with my wife, and she'll be good company for you."

"In any case, you have no choice," added Derek in that same, grim tone.

Cathy gave a little sigh. She knew when she was outvoted. They'd never leave her here. Indeed, she didn't want to be left. She started to move toward the door, knowing that if she dallied, Derek would probably take great pleasure in subjecting her to the humiliation of throwing her over his shoulder caveman-style and carrying her out. It would be just like him! She reached for the blanket she had dropped in her earlier struggles against him. She needed it to wrap around her shoulders like a shawl under the thin old extra raincoat she'd taken earlier from the peg by the door. Shivering a little, she moved between them and left the lodge.

Lashed by the rains that seemed to have intensified, the three bent almost double as they moved against the wind and water. Grimacing with distaste, Cathy slogged through ankle-deep muck to a large four-wheel-drive vehicle.

As she approached, she saw two other men waiting inside. Both stared at her with open curiosity. These men probably believed she and Derek were lovers, and assumed she had spent the night in this secluded lodge by choice rather than necessity. With a sigh, she slid out of the wet, useless raincoat and into the back of the car in one quick movement. She shifted across the seat and wrapped the blanket more tightly around her. Derek followed, squeezing in beside her on the narrow, equipment-cluttered seat.

"We're dropping the young woman with my wife," announced the red-haired stranger as he settled in behind the wheel. She'll be safer there than here. Oh, by the way," he said, revving the engine, "my name is Angus MacDowell. This here's Patrick Voorstadt," he continued, nodding to the blond-haired man sitting next to him. "And Richard Farley." He tossed a glance from Derek and Cathy to the man huddled on Cathy's right. In return, Derek and Cathy introduced themselves.

For a while then there was desultory conversation about local families. The complicated net of interconnecting relationships between those who had lived on this land for several generations produced this sort of talk. How well Cathy remembered a hundred such exchanges from the past when she lived here.

"Oh, by the by," Angus turned in the driver's seat to shoot a piercing look first at Cathy, then Derek and back to Cathy again. "The missus is working at the hospital on Blantyre Road. You're a little thing. Just hope you're up to helping out there."

Cathy went rigid. *The leprosy hospital*! Angus's wife was working at the leprosy hospital. Revulsion— and shame at her revulsion—fought fiercely within her. At one time up to ten percent of the population in some areas of Africa, Central Africa especially, had been infected with leprosy, Cathy knew, just as she knew it was still a health problem in Malawi though under control. She'd followed articles chronicling the progress of the diagnosis and treatment of the disease ever since she was in her early teens and learned how widespread was the horrifying affliction. Brief association was not dangerous, but still she shuddered at the thought of going there. This rational knowledge simply couldn't stifle that age-old emotion of revulsion at picturing herself working even for a few hours at the leprosy hospital.

"*Which* hospital on Blantyre Road, Angus? There are several, you know."

Derek's question was urgent, yet calm, and Cathy was sure he'd read her mind. She dared to think she'd found more than an ally in him on this matter, she'd found a protector.

"Why, sir," Angus burst out forcefully as though he, too, had only just realized the possible mistake, "the Children's Hospital, of course!"

Cathy's sigh of relief whistled embarrassingly through the confines of the closed vehicle. And she was grateful for the slight squeeze Derek gave her hand.

"Do you remember your Nyanja, Cathy?" he asked softly. "Most of the native children who'll be in that hospital speak virtually no English. You'll be lost in helping them without their language, you know."

She nodded. "Of course I'm aware of that." Wasn't Nyanja the *lingua franca* of most of the Central and Southern parts of Malawi with Tumbuka the common language, the tongue of commerce in the northern regions? And didn't she speak it more than adequately six years ago? She grimaced and left the questions unspoken. Here she was being edgy with Derek again—and just when he'd been so ready to champion her. "I was amazed the language came flowing back the moment I stepped foot in Malawi three days ago," she said quietly. "But, then, I learned to speak it when I was *very* young."

"Yes," Derek murmured, his eyes narrowed and his expression inscrutable, "*very* young."

Uncomfortable, Cathy let her eyes drift away to study their fellow passengers. The blond-haired man introduced as Patrick Voorstadt was suntanned and hearty looking, tall like Angus but more slender. His hair had begun to gray, but it blended so nicely into the blond she hardly noticed at first. Suddenly he turned in his seat to face her and Derek. The lines crinkling around his eyes and mouth deepened as he grinned at both of them.

"I must say, lad," he addressed Derek, "you have fine taste in the ladies."

Of course his words were meant as a compliment both to Cathy's beauty and to Derek for winning her— or so the man believed.

"Yes, I've always prided myself on my taste," Derek replied blandly. "I like my women good looking."

Her jaw dropped. She wanted to protest in no uncertain terms that she was not to be considered "his woman." He met her eyes. In them she saw a smug amusement that only intensified her outrage.

Her mouth snapped shut. She opened it to draw in a breath to speak again, but Derek continued, seeming to take great delight in egging these strangers on.

"But of course she can be a *real* little devil," he added. "Such a temper!"

Cathy glared back at him with murder in her eyes. Her hand itched to wipe that smirk right off his face with a nice slap. Worse, her reaction seemed only to intensify his mirth. He barely managed to hold back his laughter. "I'll get you for this!" Not wanting to make a scene in front of these other strangers, she silently mouthed her threat. Exactly *how* she'd take her own sweet revenge, she did not know. Derek shouldn't have dared to do this; her own reputation didn't concern her much, but she did care about her uncle's feelings. She knew how close knit these local families were. Most of them probably knew her uncle—if not personally, then by name or reputation. It appalled her to think that from these three men the rumor would spread that she and Derek Guenther were lovers.

Just then Angus MacDowell turned off onto a narrow gravel-covered drive leading up toward a large, two-story stone building up the summit of a slope.

Bushes, crisp and brown from the dry season, grew close around its foundation. Beyond a small manicured front yard were the tangled vines and bushes, scrub and weeds that nature had always used to carpet this land. These mingled to form a subtle color pattern of green, brown, and yellow that seemed especially intense now that the sun's glare did not wash out their subtleties. She saw movement in one of the front windows. A second glance revealed a small calico cat whose whiskers twitched as it stared outward at the approaching Land-Rover from its own comfortable haven indoors. As they drew up, the red-haired man honked his horn in a sharp, patterned sequence. He paused and repeated the signal. A woman opened the front door and waved.

"That's my wife. Go to her, lass," Angus said, speaking in a kindly tone, "and your man will come for you when it is over."

Derek was *not* her man, she felt like shouting. Instead she merely turned to glare at him one last time and ask him to move so that she, sitting in the middle, could get out. When she saw a redoubled amusement glinting in his eyes, however, apprehension surged up in her.

Suddenly she knew he was up to something, and her eyes widened. She really couldn't believe what happened next. Without warning he reached for her, gathering her into his arms to give her a great bear hug.

"Good-bye, darling," he murmured for all the men

in the car to hear. Imprisoned by his embrace, Cathy couldn't break free without making a scene. She went limp in his arms then. "Don't worry," he went on as if consoling a frightened lover. "I'll be all right, and I can go about my task happy in knowing that you're safe and busy with something important to do here. You have no idea what a load that takes off my heart, sweet Cathy!"

She knew him well enough to catch the laughter barely suppressed in his voice. As she struggled, trying not to be obvious in her anger and therefore unpleasant around the others, she glanced sideways from under the thick, black lashes curving against her cheeks. She blushed to see how the men gazed at her and Derek with sympathy for two lovers parting under difficult circumstances.

Cathy was too well-bred to start a scene in front of strangers. But Derek would be sorry . . . oh yes, he'd pay through the nose for this!

He gave no indication of seeing her anger. The expression on his face became, if anything, more tender. Only in his eyes did she detect the mocking glint.

"I'll miss you, sweetheart," he went on, barely swallowing his laughter. Holding her firmly imprisoned, he swooped down to press his mouth to her own in a brief but tenderly passionate kiss.

The whole incident, she knew, had probably taken only a few seconds, but she felt as if long minutes had dragged by. As she fought free, Cathy drew in a deep, shuddering breath. Her lips seemed to burn. Without speaking another word, she pushed free, taking pains to trample his toes as she thrust herself out the open car door into the rain.

chapter 6

MABEL MACDOWELL WAS a pleasant, kindly-looking woman who—rather startlingly—stood a full six feet tall. Ample padding covered her big bones, giving her a formidable appearance which her mild-mannered disposition quickly banished. Tightly curled brown hair surrounded her wide, pale face. She seemed vaguely familiar. Almost at once Cathy realized where she had seen the woman before.

Mrs. MacDowell had been a friend of her Aunt Mary—Uncle Howard's wife—and had visited Africa House quite often when Cathy was a child. She'd been just another grown-up of no particular interest except as a guest who "caused" a tea party. Always when her aunt entertained, Cathy stayed around for tea because she loved the sticky-sweet goodies served to visitors, but rarely to family. The delight of biting into flaky crusted little pastries filled with red berry jam or tiny doughnuts deep fried and dusted with powdered sugar overshadowed all other impressions Cathy might have formed of those afternoon socials so long ago.

She hadn't been too much interested in any of her aunt's lady friends back then, and after a few minutes of polite, strained conversation, she realized she still had very little in common with Mabel MacDowell. She was much more drawn to the sounds of the children which echoed into the square, chilly foyer.

Mabel clasped a hand to her forehead. "Oh, but what am I doing jabbering away about nothing at all when there's the kiddies to tend and you so uncomfortable in those shorts with that wee blanket about you."

Cathy smiled. She'd hardly call the blanket "wee," though the halter beneath certainly was. "Do you think there might be something I could change into? I'd be so grateful if there were." Mabel ran her eyes appraisingly over Cathy's small, but well-rounded frame. "A nurse's uniform, perhaps?" Cathy prompted.

"Ah, yes. Without a doubt. And there I was thinking maybe I'd have to search out some of the biggest children's clothes for a little thing like you." Mabel swept her arm around Cathy's shoulder and began to steer her in the direction of a broad staircase.

"Oh, just one more thing... and the most important. Is there a phone I can use?" Cathy asked. "My uncle hasn't had word of me since I left his house yesterday well before the storm started. He's ill, you see, and I'm especially worried about how his fear for me might affect his condition."

"Poor things, both of you. And I'm afraid I've only sad news. The storm's knocked everything out of kilter. Why, the only reason we have electricity is because this is a children's hospital and my man and the other dear men round and about chipped in to buy a gasoline-powered generator. Otherwise, we'd be using hurricane lamps or candles. All the power lines are down."

"Oh, no." Cathy's heart sank. But there was nothing she could do. She was powerless.

"But wait a bit," Mabel said heartily. "I do think there's a ham radio in the office. Yes, I'm positive. They got it for just such an emergency as this storm if one of the children should need some special care. We'll go straightaway to Matron's office and see if it's working."

Cathy followed the large, friendly woman into a ground-floor wing corridor, keeping her fingers crossed that the radio would work and she'd get through to someone who knew her uncle and could get word to him.

There was no one in the office. "I'd best be warning you," Mabel told her. "It's deserted in here because there's many a child down with flu. So we're short-handed and busy as the devil. Course the tikes who aren't sick are either frightened of this rainstorm or acting up with some kind of spirit." Mabel fiddled with the dials on the radio. "What mischief those little boys and girls can make!" Her eyes twinkled and Cathy could tell the depth of the affection with which Mabel regarded the small charges in the hospital which functioned more like an orphanage and foster home than just a straight medical facility.

At last the radio sputtered to life, humming with hope to Cathy's ears. She called her message into the mike for anyone to hear. Finally, to her relief, the voice of one of her uncle's immediate neighbors crackled over the receiver. He promised that he'd get word to Howard right away that she was safe.

Cathy felt weak with relief, then almost immediately buoyed with joy. She rubbed her hands, feeling ready for anything—especially to work with the children. The face she turned to Mabel MacDowell was totally devoid of the strain that had pulled her features tight. She was glowing.

"Let's get to it. Some fresh clothes...and then those 'little tikes' you've been telling me about with their intimidating mischief-making."

Mabel chuckled. "I think we're going to be friends, my girl. Just come along this way and we'll have you at work in nothing flat!"

And so it was that in a scant few minutes Cathy found herself—garbed in a freshly starched gray uniform with a white cardigan tossed over her shoulders and squeaky white leather shoes beneath thick white stockings—in a very noisy playroom. The prancing, lively children didn't fail to notice her entrance, but neither did they allow the newcomer to interfere with their games. Cathy, left by Mabel who returned to one of the wards, looked around. She found what she sought, the few children separated from the rest, not engaged in games, but feeling, obviously, frightened and lonely. In a trice she'd gently persuaded the smaller one into her lap and drawn the other to her side. She crooned a few words to them in Nyanja to put them further at ease, then found brightly colored blocks and began to play with them. But the idyll was soon over.

A larger child was thwacking a small playmate; there were squabbles that the other woman watching the children hadn't time to deal with. There were a few hurts and scrapes, some loud wailing, and soon Cathy felt like a fireman-policeman-nurse-soother to the little people around her. It was after lunch when the real problems started however. Several of her little charges became ill. There were faces to be bathed, clothes to be changed, messes to clean up, bedpans to fetch. The flu had struck again and again.

Once, though, pausing for a breath at the window, she thought of the world outside. The early afternoon sky was almost black from the storm clouds swirling low and ominously. Trees bent under the force of the wind. Jagged bolts of lightning pierced the clouds.

She thought of Derek and the other men. They'd be filling and piling sandbags at the riverbank to block the churning, storm-frothed waters. There were homes and farms along the Shire that would be wiped out. People hurt. Derek. The image of him being hurt, or worse, was sudden, and so painful it might have been real. She turned abruptly from the window. But the small, dark child who whimpered for her attention only made the painful knot in her stomach tighten. The dark, huge eyes were full of misery. And not only did Cathy feel for the little fellow and rush to bathe his hot forehead, but she knew a new and different sensation. A stab of desire to have a child of her own...and Derek's. The poignant realization almost took her breath away, and she trembled with the depth and profundity of her desire.

But it was shortly after a tea break that afternoon that she knew another emotion just as great. She was just turning to go up the broad staircase when she heard something that made her stop cold and listen intently.

"Things're really bad." The voice of a man wafted up to her clear and loud. From its somber tone she sensed his anxiety, and she knew the man was talking about the storm. Alarmed, Cathy stopped short to listen.

"Well, has anyone been hurt?" That was Mabel MacDowell's voice and the tone revealed the worried, fearful concern of a devoted wife waiting for news of her husband.

"No...not that we know of, thank God, though a few cattle have been washed up drowned."

"What about Angus?" The woman's voice dropped low in breathless urgency.

"I cannot lie to you, Mrs. MacDowell. He's down

where it's really rough; but you know, the man has brains. He'll not take any unnecessary chances."

"*Unnecessary* chances!" She spoke those two words with odd intensity. Cathy shuddered. Derek, for all his faults, had never been a coward. Though he'd avoid foolish, needless risks, he wouldn't shy away from doing anything he considered necessary.

In the heat and passion of storm and river rising, endangering homes and perhaps lives, how far would he go? With a pang she thought of the way she had left him, glaring into his eyes. What if she never saw Derek again? What if he died out there in the storm?

The old bitterness disappeared. All that mattered now was that he, the others, too, of course, should not be hurt. The frightening thing was, they might be. The stranger bringing news to Mabel MacDowell tried hard to hide his nervousness. Cathy moved around and could see him through the opened door. Lines of exhaustion played around his eyes and mouth. He, too, had been fighting the rising river, barricading it with sandbags and rocks. The others had sent him to deliver word to wives and mothers, daughters, and sisters who waited, anxious and afraid.

The man's news, redoubling Cathy's fear for Derek's safety, brought a stunning pulse-pounding awareness of how limited was her view of him in the past. He might have lied to her about his reasons for never coming to the hospital those years ago. Now she could understand all the good reasons for believing his explanations.

She glanced uneasily toward the man trying to re-assure Mabel. The hollowness of his tone told a story different from his actual words.

"Where are they now?" Mabel asked in a shaky voice.

"About a mile down, right on the banks," replied the man.

At once Cathy knew what she must do. She under-stood that she must go to Derek, beg his forgiveness for her closed mind. It might be too soon to secure his love, but she knew it was time to listen to him. For the sake of both their past love and perhaps even of a future for them, she must let go of her self-centered perspective. Had she ever appraised the situation calmly instead of through a tear-filled haze of hurt and recrimination? Had she ever really tried to discover and understand what had motivated Derek's actions?

Come hell or the high water already swelling over the river's banks, she must find Derek and confess her uncertainty, her willingness to listen—and to forgive. She had to go! Now!

Fortunately neither Mabel nor the man had noticed her. If they found out she was going out into the storm, they'd stop her, so she took care to be very quiet.

She couldn't find much in the way of raingear in the back entry, only a torn oilcloth poncho. She wasn't deterred. She was too anxious to find Derek and set things right between them. Bare-headed she darted out the back door of the hospital.

Rain lashed at her. The storm roared around her with fierce intensity. She looked back at the warm and well-lit building and felt a pang. The storm was nasty. But she had to get to Derek. She half ran down the hill onto the road, then beyond it to where a short distance away she knew the river assaulted its high banks. The wind blew against her but she forced herself forward toward the river and most importantly toward that part of the river where Derek and the others struggled to hold back the flood. She was driven on by her need to see him, to rectify her mistakes.

She wasn't afraid for herself. All of the land around here, particularly along the Shire River, had been settled for generations. It was farmland or grazing pasture for domesticated livestock. And far off, forty or so miles away, Tanyasi was well fenced in by barbed wire and natural obstacles. No wild animals would be prowling around to endanger her with fangs and claws.

She moved along purposefully. No matter what else, those wild jeep rides with Derek so many years earlier had left her with a pretty good feeling for the lay of the land. She recognized familiar landmarks.

Pellets of rain stung her skin. The wind, screaming hard past her, whipped and tore at the poncho. She struggled against its force. From the conversation she'd overheard, she knew the greatest danger lay further south, maybe half a mile beyond where the road curved, then started downhill. Sticking to the road's paved surface as long as she could, head lowered, bent almost double against the wind, Cathy pushed forward until at last reaching that point where she must leave the road.

Fighting the wind's resistance, she stood straight.

Turning toward the river, she tried to peer through the almost solid wall of water flowing down to what lay beyond. Her view was blocked. Trees, rocks, grasses, and most of all the weather itself, gray and solid yet constantly moving—obscured her vision. Her wet hair was a burden on her neck and shoulders. And the water-soaked clothes flattened to her body by the virtually useless poncho felt like liquid ice on her skin.

Bracing herself, she stepped from the road into the tall undergrowth. She cringed but did not stop as whipping, cordlike grasses slashed the white stockings to ribbons around her legs. Somewhere in the back of her mind she knew that tiny lines like cat scratches marked her legs.

As she turned to her right, she saw the river looming out of the gray mist. In dry season it flowed sluggishly as a calm ribbon of sky-reflecting water. Years, and perhaps centuries, of its passage had cut a shallow valley into the underlying soil and rocks. Most of the time this easily contained its flow. Today, however, the river roared. Its waters had swollen. It churned violently. White foam flecked its blackish waters. Cathy stood, staring in fascination at the countless eddies and swirls within the greater torrent.

The normally placid river seemed to scream an angry threat of death to anyone who dared approach. She felt its power in the ground itself vibrating up through the soles of her feet. Its fury was hypnotic. Where was Derek, upriver now or below? She glanced helplessly in both directions. Whatever way she chose would probably prove wrong.

With a resigned sigh, she started downriver, following its swollen course. She had walked a long, long time battling wind and storm in her desperation to find her way to Derek. Uncertain now that she was even going in the right direction, she began to feel her exhaustion. Her mind focused only on her dogged determination to continue. In any case she had no choice. With the storm raging, she could hardly stay here by the water's edge.

Tiredness made her clumsy. She did not realize how dangerous this could be until her foot caught in the upward gnarl of a half-buried root of a knobthorn tree. Normally she would have been able to catch her balance and go on, but her reflexes were too slow from fatigue. She took a hard, brutal, sprawling fall. And it was the last straw!

She crawled to the nearest tree, a great, friendly looking baobob, and sat with her back against the trunk. She turned her face up and closed her eyes. The branches above sheltered her from the worst of the rain. She breathed heavily. The light in her mind was dimming, almost flickering out. The roaring of the river seemed far away.

chapter 7

CATHY, HALF DREAMING, remembered a poem she'd learned in high school. She didn't even remember its title, only its story. There was a ship at sea, a terrible storm and the captain's beautiful daughter was lashed to the mainmast to protect her. The girl was protected from the sea all right, but not the other elements. After the storm, she was found dead, frozen to the mast. Somehow in her mind Cathy became that captain's daughter, rigid and blue beneath covered ropes. It seemed so real, so vivid that she could see that old New England schooner and see, too, herself bound and helpless.

Suddenly from afar she heard faint shouting. Human voices yelled and called, but she was too far gone to do anything but acknowledge inwardly that she had heard them. She wondered dimly if, like travelers lost in the desert seeing a mirage, there could be such hallucinations with sound instead of vision. She had passed, however, beyond caring. The shouts grew louder. Over the storm she heard someone yelling. Dimly she acknowledged the presence of a man splashing toward her. She felt him close by. His strong arm slipped around her.

"Cathy . . . Cathy, darling!" She recognized Derek's voice. It seemed to be coming from a great distance, but in truth he was shouting right in her ear. Consciousness began sifting back. A cold, gray daylight surrounded her again. Her eyes opened, with lashes fluttering, upon badly focused figures who stood over her.

She blinked. Derek was holding her in his arms. His body warmed her. His touch soothed and exhilarated her. "Derek!" she whispered. She raised one hand to touch his cheek, then almost immediately dropped it back down, shocked at how tired she was.

He picked her up and she clung to him with arms wrapped around his neck, savoring his warmth as much as the feel of his body. He carried her a short distance to some boulders jutting within view of the river, but up a slight incline. As he drew close, she saw that the largest of these had fused, becoming a tiny cave. Only when he had reached it did Derek lower her down safe in its shelter.

"Oh, Cathy!" Derek clasped her in a tight embrace. Even his very touch radiated love, passion, sincerity. At once all the years of pain seemed unimportant. As if suffering a terrible nightmare, she had awakened to find it fading into nothing more than a dim memory.

She felt now with a burst of joy that Derek loved her. He always had, no matter what anyone had told her to the contrary. He would *never* have gone away and abandoned her, at least not the way she had been led to believe—by choice. No matter what her uncle and the others had told her, Derek would have come if he could have to that hospital in Blantyre.

Gasping, Derek suddenly drew back. "Here you are, freezing, and I do nothing to help you."

"Derek, it's all right." She wanted him to hold her close, not pull away. His very touch warmed her now. She felt so glad just to be with him, and so thankful both of them were alive.

She leaned where he had propped her back against the cave wall. She still felt so weak, so yielding, almost as if she were floating. She watched him with fascination as he reached again for some clothes, just now noticing the bundle he had carried along with her in his arms to this sheltered spot. "These aren't much in the way of looks," he said, "but they'll keep you warmer than those soaking things you've got on."

He unfolded a flannel shirt printed in a rather hideous red, green, and black plaid pattern. It was huge, almost enough to wrap twice around her, but the heavy fuzzy weave of it looked warm.

"Get dressed," he said, nodding to the pile of clean,

dry clothes. She felt too exhausted. "Get dressed, Cathy," he repeated, frowning now.

She didn't feel like moving. She was so happy just basking in her own joy at finding him, and herself, alive and well. "Derek," she murmured, smiling at him through misty eyes. "I was so afraid for you. I— I came to find you."

"Cathy, later! The important thing now is to get you into dry clothes before you catch pneumonia."

Oh, couldn't he see it didn't matter? Nothing mattered now but the happiness and delight she felt in savoring his presence. Who cared that she shivered a little? Certainly not her. Love alone could warm her.

Derek, however, was determined to play the parent role, or so it seemed. Though it irritated Cathy just a little, she did not resist as he reached for her, pulling off the poncho and the sodden cardigan. Perhaps deep down she had wanted all along for him to do just that. She shivered to feel his fingers curl around the buttons of the wet uniform. Smiling, she stroked his cheek as he reached to pull it off. As he moved, undressing her, he seemed very grim and serious all of a sudden. He spoke with an explosive burst that alarmed her. "You shouldn't have come, Cathy. You should have stayed with Mabel MacDowell and the children."

Passive in exhaustion, she let him coax her arms back to strip off the dress. "But the children are well taken care of," she murmured. "I was at tea . . . and other women had come to help."

Cold air chilled her flesh. Strangely excited to be naked in his presence, Cathy clung to him. Hungrily she resisted all his attempts to dress her. She knew that when he did, he'd leave her alone again. She did not want that. She ached to linger right there in his arms forever.

"Derek, maybe you're right about how I should have stayed put, but I couldn't. I was so afraid for you," she went on, trying to explain more fully her complicated, mixed feelings, "so afraid that I'd never get the chance to know for sure why things went wrong."

Gently, with obvious regret, he disentangled himself from her embrace. "You almost didn't." His brows had raised above eyes gone tenderly serious. "Had you waited where you belonged, none of this would have happened."

"I couldn't stand it," she whispered back at him, "staying there, not knowing. I . . . I went a little mad, I suppose."

"A little mad? Completely crazy running out into the storm. You nearly got yourself killed, you little idiot." In his eyes, however, she saw a look of wonderment.

His gaze dropped. For the first time he seemed to notice how she clung in his arms, bare-chested. Involuntarily he drew in a sharp breath. "Oh, Cathy!" he gasped.

Forgetting the storm, forgetting the cold, Cathy reached for him. Holding his hand in her now trembling one, she raised it to chest level, then pushed it, palm downward, upon the spot where her breasts pressed together. Her move was not an invitation, but a demand.

Derek's lips parted. He drew in a low, shuddering

breath. A wild, hungry light glinted in his eyes. His gaze burned into her. His very way of looking at her devoured her. "My God!" he muttered. His hand lingered. The other reached behind to draw her closer. Pressed against him, she felt through her own chest the wild pounding of Derek's heart. She sensed his desperate, rising hunger. His passion heated and hardened and focused his male energy. Its very force and presence promised to possess her, to satisfy her yearning needs as nothing else could.

She gasped. Her mouth craved the taste of his kisses. She ached to lose herself forever in the delicious warmth of his love and passion.

He too seemed to have forgotten time and place. His arms held her. His embrace possessed her. One hand slid down her back, the other up into her hair, exploring every sweet, soft inch of her. Each deep, shuddering breath he took reassured her of his need for her. He lowered his face to her own, pressing a deep yet tender kiss upon her lips.

He savored for a long time the honeyed sweetness of her mouth. The wild pounding of her own heart pressed so close to his must surely have signaled to him her eager, welcoming response. His arms closed around her as she writhed in his embrace. He must have sensed how she ached to begin and finish what they had not known from one another in years. His knowing, loving caress aroused her to a fever pitch of readiness. Sweet memories mingled now with anticipation. Moaning aloud, she clung to him with flesh afire, ready, willing, waiting.

"Now. Please, Derek, now!" Hungrily she nibbled kisses all over him. Her mouth slid forward. With face and nose pressed inward against the side of his head, she inhaled deeply to enjoy again the clean, soap-scented fragrance of his wild blond hair.

Suddenly, however, Derek drew back. "Cathy!" he gasped. "This is insane!" His eyes skimmed over her nakedness again. This time horror mingled with his desire. "*I* must be insane to let this go on."

His hand trembled as he reached for the flannel shirt. Very gently but with firm insistence he guided her arms into its huge, overlong sleeves. "Here you are half-frozen to death after a helluva time in that storm, and I just sit here..." His voice quivered as it trailed off.

"No...no!" she murmured, reaching out to him. Determined to keep him close, she used everything she had. The kiss she gave him shattered all his re-solve. Time, place, and even the desperation of their situation faded. The passion overwhelming them both swept everything else away. Nothing mattered. Nothing seemed quite real but the warmth of flesh against flesh and the tenderness of the caresses each gave the other. Happily, and with soul-deep joy Cathy gave herself up to the moment's final crowning glory.

chapter 8

IT WAS WELL after dark when they finally reached Africa House. Cathy rode with Derek and the other men in the back seat of the car that had taken them to Mabel at the Children's Hospital. The storm had subsided as darkness fell, bringing peace. To their relief the river had swelled no higher than the sandbags they had piled along its banks. They could rest easy knowing the homes they had worked so hard to save were out of danger, at least for the time being.

In the dark Cathy and Derek held hands. They talked little because both of them were exhausted, yet deeply content. More than once Cathy's eyelids dropped into the beginning of slumber. She'd find herself nodding, or she'd suddenly jerk awake to feel her head resting heavily on Derek's shoulder. Their eyes would meet and he'd smile down at her.

When the jeep finally pulled into her uncle's driveway, Cathy felt a sense of loss parting from Derek. With a listless gesture, she reached for the car door handle. "Thank you for driving me home," she murmured, glancing at the big red-haired man behind the wheel. She seemed hardly able to gather the strength anymore to speak. Even though she hadn't eaten since breakfast, the thought of food seemed less appealing than sleep. She wanted only to change into her nightgown and fall into bed. Nothing else sounded quite so good.

"I'll be in touch, Cathy," Derek spoke softly, gently, lovingly. "I'll call you tomorrow."

Her eyes misted. She turned quickly to the others. "It was nice meeting you all, though I could have wished for better circumstances." It took all her strength just to extend that final pleasantry. Without waiting for their replies, she slipped from the car to find herself standing on legs that suddenly trembled.

"Do you need any help?" Derek called after as she stepped into the mucky ground. The rain had become a steady but mild patter, more annoying now than terrifying.

"No, I'll be all right." Cathy smiled back at him, then half stumbled toward the house. She saw lights on and felt a pang of warmth to know that Mr. and

Mrs. Franklin and maybe even her uncle were up and waiting for her.

More than once since returning here she had mentally blessed the Franklins. They could have quit when Uncle Howard became ill, but they stayed on. Cathy needed help with the myriad details of running Tanyasi, so they were invaluable. What a welcome sight they'd be now!

As she approached, the door swung open. The Franklins waited eagerly as she walked toward them. Electric lights flooded the usually dim entranceway.

"Thank goodness you're all right," Mrs. Franklin cried out as her husband rushed to help Cathy inside. Nearly collapsing, she let them lead her to the kitchen where she sank at once into a chair.

"Poor child, you look ready to drop!" Mrs. Franklin handed Cathy a cup of jasmine tea already brewed, steaming hot and fragrant.

"I am," she replied, sighing. She really preferred going straight to bed, but knew the Franklins wanted to hear about what happened. "Did you get my message?" She lifted reddened eyes to them both as she asked after the one she had contacted on the radio.

In unison they nodded. "Yes, and what a blessing, it was too, to hear you were safe and well under the wing of Mabel MacDowell!"

Cathy smiled to herself but dared not admit the truth about how she had ended up spending her day!

"How did it happen?" Mrs. Franklin stared, with vague uneasiness showing in her face.

Head nodding, Cathy explained as tersely as was polite about the engine of her Land-Rover and her fortunate rescue. Leaving out those details that would only upset them, Cathy went on to describe the accident that left her stranded. She mentioned Derek Guenther, however, and his name caused the Franklins to glance uneasily at one another.

Mr. Franklin leaned toward her, frowning as he spoke. "Your uncle will be very glad to see you, Cathy, and very grateful that you were rescued, but if I were you, I'd not tell him about Derek Guenther. Gloss over it when speaking to him. You know how your uncle feels about that lad."

Cathy frowned. "He's no lad. Not anymore." She clamped her mouth tight to still any further words. She didn't want to hide her association with Derek—not when it was just beginning to flower again, yet she was uncertain about how to proceed. "Yes, but surely under the circumstances..."

"Your uncle's taken a turn for the worse, child." Very gently Mrs. Franklin interrupted her. "He's quite fragile right now."

"Oh, no!" Cathy's heart sank. She loved her uncle. If she hadn't gone out and gotten herself stranded, would her uncle's condition have remained stable?

As if sensing her thoughts, however, Mr. Franklin hastened to reassure her. "He took sick just after you left, *before* you turned up missing. It wasn't you who did it."

Cathy sighed in relief. "Can I go to him?" she whispered. Though she was so exhausted she felt ready to collapse, she wanted to visit her uncle just long enough to let him see for himself that she was all right. "I'll take your advice about not mentioning Derek," she promised.

She clung to the banister going upstairs. In the darkened hallway she saw immediately that her uncle's door was open. Through it glowed the light from his small table lamp. He lay there with a paperback book propped on his chest, but she could tell he wasn't really reading.

"Uncle Howard?"

The old man glanced in her direction, then smiled. With a feeble gesture he beckoned her in. "Glad you're back with us, Cathy," he murmured.

She returned his smile, knowing hers was equally wan. "I'm sorry I made you worry, Uncle Howard." Her voice came out barely audible. She saw, with relief, that her uncle's condition seemed stable. "I wouldn't have gotten stranded for the world," she said with a touch of humor, "if I could have avoided it."

"I know." Howard's eyes twinkled. "Sometimes everything gets beyond our control." He gave a little grimace.

For him, Cathy knew, *everything* had been out of control lately. To a man like her uncle—strong and used to being in charge—this debilitating illness must be close to intolerable.

Briefly she described what had happened, remembering the Franklins' warning. She carefully pruned certain details of her adventure, including and especially the fact that her rescuer had been none other than Derek Guenther. When she had finished apologizing with genuine regret for ruining an expensive vehicle, her uncle dismissed it all with a wave of his hand.

"Life's too short to worry about things like that, honey," he said. "When the weather's better, I'll send Raymond out to bring it back. Hopefully we can fix it. If not..." His voice trailed off into a shrug.

Cathy smiled. She knew that if anyone could repair that Land-Rover, her uncle's native-born mechanic, Raymond Oladopupo could. He'd grown up in a nearby tribal village and had an ingrained genius for understanding all things mechanical.

"Cathy, I've been meaning to tell you something... Well, even before you came over here, I'd intended to write about it. But you know how I hate to put bad news in a letter. Then you arrived and I was so happy to see you I forgot to deliver it in person. Well, anyway, what I have to tell you is bad news from my point of view." A frown plowed a deeper furrow into her uncle's brow. His eyes snapped in her direction. Their dark pupils fixed on her, suddenly intent. "It seems a certain person returned to our area, someone whose presence back here concerns me..."

She tried to be evasive. "A lot of people come and go."

"Cathy!" He rasped out her name like a command to silence. She almost recoiled from the expression on his face. Whatever she did, she'd try to get out of admitting that she had actually seen Derek. And, of course, her uncle would *never* hear a word about spending the night with him. The Franklins were right.

She had experienced firsthand in the past—and now—how much her uncle seemed to detest Derek, though she didn't understand why, and she wanted nothing to upset his fragile condition. She decided at once to put her quite genuine weariness to good use.

"Uncle Howard," she murmured, letting her eyelids droop, "I love you and I want to answer all of your questions, I even want to hear this piece of bad news of yours. But not tonight! If I don't get to bed right now, I'll collapse. And I just *don't* think poor Mr. Franklin has the strength anymore to carry me."

Her uncle gave a short bark of a laugh. "Not at *his* age. You go on, honey. We'll talk in the morning."

On suddenly trembling legs Cathy stood, then bent to kiss him on the forehead. As she did, she nearly lost her balance again.

"Yes, go to bed," Howard repeated, smiling gently up at her. "Rest. It's enough for me to know you've returned safe and well. Anything else is secondary."

Cathy awakened the next day with a bad case of the sniffles. Despite her physical discomfort, however, she felt elated because she remembered Derek's words last night—his promise to call her today. Probably over the phone he'd make arrangements to meet her again. She thought longingly of the time they had spent together in the cave, then smiled. She tingled all over just at the very memory of it. If only she didn't have a scratchy throat, everything would be perfect. She reflected, grinning, that such a minor aggravation hardly mattered.

Sniffling and blowing her nose almost constantly, but in an incredibly cheerful mood, Cathy went downstairs, and although she could not taste her food, she dived at once, with ravenous appetite, into the huge English-style breakfast Mrs. Franklin had prepared. While she ate, she glanced out the window, relieved to see a weak, watery sunshine beaming through patches of blue sky. Sipping a second cup of coffee, she wondered idly when Derek would call. With her cold and an aching body, she wanted to go back to bed and nap until the worst of it had passed. She didn't want to be half asleep or groggy from cold medicine when she talked to him again. She wished now she had pinned him down a little more concerning the time of his call.

After eating and helping Mrs. Franklin clear the table, Cathy moved to the well-heated parlor to read a while before deciding what to do. She was sitting there alone, swallowing cold medicine and overdosing on vitamin C tablets when Mrs. Franklin stepped into the room. "Cathy," she said, speaking with odd expression on her face, "you have a *visitor*."

At once Cathy's heart leaped, then seemed to plunge. With a dismayed little sound she leaped to her feet. "He came here?" she whispered. "Oh, no!" She stared at the old woman, appalled yet eager. The passion she and Derek had shared still seemed very close and wonderfully intense. Yet he should have known better than to come here. Her mind seemed to be spinning at lightning speed.

She had yearned to see him again, but not here and

not until her uncle was physically recovered from his relapse, and better able to take the news of her renewed alliance with Derek.

Nor did she care to let Derek see her the way she was dressed in comfortable but unbecoming clothes. Worst of all, her eyes were bloodshot and tearing. Her nose had swollen red from the friction of too many tissues squeezed against it. Her hair hung tangled and exasperatingly limp. She was not exactly the picture of beauty, she thought ruefully, and what girl wants the man she loves to see her at her very worst?

"Tell him," she gasped. "Tell him I'm sick and not seeing anybody." Her voice was incredibly hoarse.

"*Him*?" Mrs. Franklin's brows rose. Her voice took on a slightly frosty tone as she glanced at Cathy with a knowing, disapproving expression. "I'm sure you'll be relieved to know your caller is a woman, not whatever gentleman you were expecting."

Cathy started in surprise, then flushed with relief. Perversely, however, she felt just a little disappointed too. "Who is she?"

In a somewhat better humor Mrs. Franklin shrugged. "I really have no idea," she replied, obviously bewildered. "Her name is Mrs. Windon, if *that* gives you a clue. Frankly I've never heard of her, though I must say she appears quite *substantial*."

By "substantial" Cathy knew the grandmotherly woman did not mean that the mysterious Mrs. Windon was overweight! Well off, respectable, a woman of wealth and social standing was "substantial" in Mrs. Franklin's vocabulary. Cathy had never heard of Mrs.

Windon either. Overcome with curiosity to see who she might be, she glanced at her clothes and decided that they were probably good enough for her unexpected caller. In any case, she thought to herself, people who dropped by unannounced deserved whatever they encountered.

She turned to Mrs. Franklin now and smiled. "Well, you might as well send her on in and we can both see who she is and what she wants. I'm sure she's here for some good reason, though heaven only knows what it can be."

Within a half minute or so, Mrs. Franklin ushered the mysterious Mrs. Windon in. Cathy heard the crackling contralto voice even before she saw the woman. She stood up and moved to greet her visitor.

Mrs. Windon was a tall, striking-looking woman in her midfifties. "Elegant" would have been the one word Cathy might have used to describe her. She carried herself like a grand duchess. Perfectly coiffed gray hair framed her long, well-boned face. Her features were strong but not coarse. She had a large nose, a wide mouth, and intelligent blue eyes that peered at Cathy with disconcerting directness. As she approached, she extended one lean, well-manicured hand in greeting.

"I'm so *happy* to meet you." The woman boomed out her words the way she probably boomed out everything she said, but it was cheerful, not harsh. Even if she spoke barely above a whisper, Mrs. Windon's voice, because of its nature, probably could have projected and filled up a room much larger than the little parlor of Africa House. Hers was the voice of a stage actress, and indeed, as she swept into the room, moving closer, she advanced with such graceful self-assurance that she looked as if she belonged on stage.

"Mrs. Windon." Feeling a little awkward, Cathy was at a loss for words. Almost from first glance she had taken an instant liking to this tall, self-possessed, seemingly good-natured woman. "I'm so happy we could meet, though I must admit I have no idea what this is all about." Cathy could think of nothing else to say.

"Of *course* you don't," the woman replied reassuringly but not too helpfully. She smiled again as she liberated Cathy's fingers from her own firm but ladylike grip.

Cathy motioned her guest to sit, and Mrs. Windon settled herself with graceful ease upon one of Uncle Howard's sturdy, well-stuffed chairs. The simplicity of Mrs. Windon's gray wool dress signaled it was from a couturier who took pride in cut and design.

Mrs. Windon's slender fingers were covered with rings. Although Cathy knew almost nothing about gems, she sensed that these were genuine. No fake opal ever captured the flash and fire of the real stone, no glass could hold the glitter of diamonds or the dazzle of sapphires.

Not only in her clothes and jewels, but in her speech and carriage, too, Mrs. Windon gave off an aura of quality. Cathy tried not to stare as she waited for this sophisticated stranger to reveal the cause of her visit.

Mrs. Franklin left to bring tea. Once alone, the

woman smiled at Cathy. "I know you must be *bursting* with curiosity to know why a stranger you've never even heard of would come to call." As Cathy smiled, nodding agreement, Mrs. Windon glanced around. "Do you mind *terribly* if I smoke?" she asked, almost apologetically.

Cathy wasn't one to forbid others the pleasure of their bad habits. She smiled back, then reached behind to a nearby table for one of her uncle's ashtrays. The woman thanked her with obvious relief and opened her small Hermès handbag. She pulled out a half-used package of English Ovals and a gold lighter trimmed in tigereye.

Only after she had drawn in her first, grateful inhalation did the woman resume speaking. "I come well recommended, I hope." Her eyes met Cathy's. "Derek Guenther sent me...so to speak." Seeing Cathy's startled expression, she went on. "I suppose I ought to explain." She paused for a second, studying Cathy with just the faintest hint of narrowed eyes. But then the subtle shifting of mood passed. "Derek and I go back a long way—to when he was a boy, actually. I was the one who encouraged him to try his luck in Johannesburg."

"You?" Cathy stared. She had never heard of this woman. As Cathy waited, at a loss for words and quite surprised, the woman continued.

"He came to me last night, told me about you, and what had happened...*almost* everything." Her eyes darted a glance so knowing that Cathy realized Mrs.

Windon had probably guessed at whatever Derek might have censored.

"Oh, please, *don't*!" The woman seemed obviously dismayed. "I didn't mean to upset you, really. I wouldn't have brought it up at all except that he seemed so changed. After that last time, after you went away, he had been so bitter about you, about your uncle, your whole family in fact. But then last night he came to me, and he seemed so, well, softened."

Cathy smiled. Her cheeks glowed warmly. "Really?"

"His bitterness—"

"Oh, it's all right!" With a wave of her hand Cathy dismissed all further apologies and explanations. She turned to the older woman now with a happy smile. "I suppose he had good reason for feeling that way. Some things happened—bad things—and both of us ended up believing the worst of one another, but all that is over now." Cathy frowned, wishing to herself that she could make her Uncle Howard see how futile it was to go on feeling as he did about Derek Guenther. If only she could make him understand how deeply she loved the man he despised.

"Cathy!" The woman's voice resonated with sympathy. "This all started before you and Derek ever met. Your families—" Her voice trailed off. Her brow furrowed into a frown.

Mrs. Franklin returned carrying a tea tray. She set it down and smiled shyly. Even though Cathy invited her to remain, she refused, politely closing the door behind her.

Mrs. Windon continued. "It was a local scandal, really. Your two families—yours and his—always had bad blood between them. That's why things were made so difficult for you two."

Cathy frowned. "But why?"

"I can't really say," Mrs. Windon replied. "As you well know, certain subjects are simply not spoken about. I will tell you one thing, however, and I tell you only because knowing might help you in some way. Tanyasi, with Africa House, too, used to belong to Derek's family."

Cathy blinked in shocked surprise. "I never knew *that*!"

The woman shrugged. "It was way back, of course, before Derek's father gambled away his fortune, but there was always ill feeling about losing it. No one ever wanted to discuss it."

Cathy's head reeled. "That explains something, I'm sure, though I don't know exactly what." She raised her eyes to the woman. "I knew Derek was poor but..." She shook her head. "He's done very well for himself, hasn't he? He owns that lodge, that hideaway he took me to, doesn't he?" What had happened in Johannesburg to change Derek's fortunes so drastically?

The woman smiled as she nodded, then answered, speaking with an almost maternal pride that surprised and startled Cathy. "That and quite a good-sized estate nearby, as well as some office buildings and apartments in Blantyre. He has a flat in one of them, I believe, a penthouse, though I've never seen it. He doesn't seem to like it much, nor city living either. Since coming back, he spends as much time at the lodge as possible. He's been dreadfully involved with business lately and unable to get out there. And angry as a scalded cat about that, too!"

The extent of Derek's wealth shocked Cathy. "How in the world did he manage such success in so short a time?" she gasped, blurting the question out.

The woman shrugged. "You know Derek at least well enough to understand that he is very intelligent, talented, strong willed."

Cathy could not argue with any of those descriptions. She merely nodded and smiled as the woman went on. "Well, I suppose some of it was luck, getting noticed by the right people, coming up with the right idea at the right time. I backed his first mining venture and it was one of the best investments I ever made. In any case, he did very well for himself in Johannesburg."

"I got the strong impression he hated it there," Cathy murmured, more to herself than to her visitor.

"Oh, yes! Yes, he hated it with a passion, but be that as it may, the town proved to be his own personal El Dorado, and he had the brains and the drive to take advantage. He left after you two parted, as I said, at my encouragement. I saw he needed to get away from his painful memories, and being older and wiser, I pointed out a good avenue for him. Anyway he ended up owning interests in a couple of mines, but always," she added sighing, "always his heart was in Malawi, and he came back here as soon as he could."

The woman crushed out her cigarette, then leaned

toward Cathy. She spoke with almost disconcerting directness. "But of course none of this explains my surprise visit to you this morning, does it? I must apologize, really, for not giving you warning, but I'm afraid I don't always behave in as well-bred a fashion as I ought."

Amused by her visitor's flippant comment, Cathy smiled, then murmured the expected denial.

"The fact is, dear, there wasn't really time with the phone lines all awry because of the storm. I'm having an open house Saturday evening and would like you to come. My home isn't outrageously far from here, and if the weather turns nasty, it's spacious enough to accommodate whoever needs to stay over."

Her smile warmed Cathy.

"I've heard so much about you from Derek and from others. I really would like you to join us. You can't possibly know many families around here...not after all these years, and it will give you a chance to get reacquainted. Derek will be there too," she added. "No doubt he'll get in touch with you himself today. You *must* come to my party!"

"I-I'd love to," Cathy stammered, "but I might not be able to. My uncle's health is precarious, and he took a turn for the worse a day or so ago."

"Well, the invitation holds, no matter what. And even if you can't make it, I hope to see you again." She rose. "Derek would probably be appalled to learn I actually took the liberty of dropping by like this. I hope your uncle feels better, at least well enough so that your housekeeper can look after him for one night." Within minutes the woman was gone, leaving in her wake the scent of expensive perfume mingled with burnt tobacco.

All that day Howard seemed to hold his own if not improve. He did not press Cathy for details concerning her rescue, and she did not offer any. As she sat by his bedside, however, reading aloud to him on what had turned into another rainy afternoon, she felt his eyes upon her, studying her as if in spite of everything, he knew.

Late that afternoon the phone rang. Her uncle took the call before she could get to the instrument. He smiled at her with an oddly triumphant expression on his face. "We'll be having a visitor tonight for dinner," he announced.

Cathy's eyes widened. "A visitor? Are you sure you're well enough?"

"I feel much better."

"Who then?"

"Syd Schaeffer."

"Oh!" Cathy's heart sank. Syd Schaeffer was one of her uncle's former business associates. He had inherited two factories in Blantyre and a plantation on the far side of the Shire River. Though in his midthirties, Syd had never married. Instead of children, he raised Pomeranians, tiny high-strung dogs with squashed-in faces and moppy tails. He was an extremely pleasant man. Cathy had known him since she was a teen-ager. Syd had always liked her, more than liked her, she knew, because of the special way he'd always looked at her with mingled desire and a patronizing tenderness. "Just wait until you grow up," he teasingly threatened long ago.

At her uncle's instigation, Cathy had no doubt, Syd had met her at the airport. And, probably also at her uncle's instigation, he'd hinted even that first day of reacquaintance that he believed she'd make a very fine wife.

Cathy had never been the slightest bit interested in Syd. Unfortunately her uncle liked and approved of Syd Schaeffer and seemed subtly to push him and the subject of marriage just in this short time she'd been home again in Africa House. Now that her mind and heart lingered upon Derek Guenther with longing, hungry anticipation of the joy they would soon know in one another's arms, dealing with poor Syd would be incredibly difficult. Indeed she'd probably need all her willpower just to hide her irritation with him.

"Be nice to Syd, Cathy." Her uncle's tired old eyes fixed on her now with a surprisingly intent and, she thought, cunning expression.

Cathy sighed. "I am nice to everyone, Uncle Howard." She forced a smile as she turned to leave. Syd would never, could never overpower her the way Derek did. He would never be capable of arousing any deeper emotion in her than annoyance.

Derek's very ability to provoke her to heights of anger as well as bliss was what gave their relationship its bite and sizzle. She wished she knew someone with whom to talk over her feelings. Back in the States she had women friends to confide in, but not here.

"Look *pretty* for him, Cathy," continued her uncle.

At once her heart sank. Turning back to him, she tried to make light of his request. "I *always* try to look attractive, Uncle Howard," she said, smiling at him.

"*You* know what I mean." He spoke with such a grave tone her heart sank. "Give him a chance, Cathy," he urged. "I'd like to see you safe before I go."

Cathy felt a pang. She and her uncle shared rich memories of many happy times together. The thought of his declining health, his impending death brought her terrible pain. She felt, too, a twinge of resentment that he'd use guilt to try and pressure her into something she didn't want. Worse, she sensed all too well how that casting of guilt would probably intensify if and when he found out about her and Derek.

On impulse she turned back to him. She could not live a lie, not even for him. "Uncle Howard," she began, "I know how you care for me and I appreciate your concern, but really being "safe" in your terms is a somewhat outmoded idea. I've loved my independence these past years. I'm twenty-six, remember? Not sixteen. And I'm not afraid of being alone." She shrugged. Confronting him was one thing. Confessing to him her feelings for Derek was more than she had nerve to do as she looked into his illness-ravaged face.

"Give Syd a chance, Cathy. That's all I ask. Give him a chance." The old man spoke to her now with strange, disturbing urgency.

She herself had other thoughts, other worries, and as she left his room, one question nagged at her with obsessive intensity. Why hadn't Derek called? What was keeping him? She'd lingered near the phone almost all day, to grab it up when it rang and thus kill any chance her uncle might have to intercept the call she longed to receive. The fact that Syd had been able to get through proved beyond doubt that the lines had been repaired. What was the problem?

chapter 9

IN SPITE OF weakness, her uncle managed to sit through dinner, presiding at the head of his table like the patriarch he had always been, with Syd seated to his right and Cathy to his left. The meal was well cooked, the atmosphere seemed pleasant enough, but was laced with tension.

With a pang she thought of another meal, one taken with Derek in the gray light of yesterday morning. It, too, had been fraught with tension and under-currents, but of a different kind, at once more promising and yet more disturbing in a way that had enlivened her. Poor Syd. She felt sorry for him. He tried so hard but failed in what Derek accomplished so effortlessly. Funny, she reflected now, Derek had even tried at times to antagonize, yet love remained, linking both of them as two souls meant to be together—no matter what the difficulties piled between them.

Syd looked so distinguished with stylishly cut hair graying just at the temples and his body kept trim from lunch hours devoted to exercises at a health club near his office; yet everything about him left her cold. Throughout the meal his soft brown eyes fixed longingly upon her, annoying her. They seemed to melt right into her in a way that reminded her of sticky candy. It was easy enough, too, whenever she met those eyes, to turn quickly away, though he usually moved first, as if ashamed to be caught by her glance.

A fleeting frown furrowed her brow, then disappeared. There had to be good reasons why Derek hadn't called. Perhaps he felt unwilling to expose her to her uncle's disapproval or further anger and weakening of his condition if the old man should find out he was in touch with her. Or maybe after yesterday's ordeal his body had simply needed more time than he had expected to recuperate. It could have been anything, any reason at all.

Cathy glanced at Syd, then quickly away, feeling yet another flash of annoyance. Something in Syd's expression made her grateful to have chosen to dress as she had. Mother-of-pearl buttons fastened her white nylon blouse to its prim little Peter Pan collar. Its fullness partially hid from view the contours of her body. Yet even so, the way his gaze sometimes lin-

gered on her bosom when he thought she wasn't looking embarrassed Cathy. Her skin heated just sensing
how his eyes, combined with his imagination, must
be savoring the warm, suntanned flesh that Derek had
kissed and caressed. That, Cathy thought, sighing, was
the *real* problem. Syd just wasn't Derek. And she
desperately wanted Derek!

Toward the end of the meal Syd changed the subject
abruptly from whatever he and her uncle had been
talking about. He turned to her. "I thought we might
go out Saturday night."

"Oh, I can't!" Startled, Cathy blurted it out, then
instantly regretted not being more evasive.

"Why not?" her uncle demanded. He leaned toward
her, staring in annoyed curiosity.

"Well, I . . . I had a caller today, someone I met
because of the flood, a very nice lady named Mrs.
Windon. She invited me over to an open house Saturday night. I was just planning to drop by . . . on my
own."

Syd spoke with an urgent, wheedling tone. "Let me
escort you there, please. You'll have a much better
time, I think, if you go with someone instead of by
yourself."

"I think that's a splendid idea!" her uncle said.
"You'll enjoy yourself if you're with someone you
know. And what better choice could you make than
Syd?" He looked at her pointedly.

To admit that she wanted to go alone so that she'd
be free to spend the evening with Derek was out of
the question. She tried to wriggle out of it.

"Oh, I can't," she replied just a little too breathlessly. "In any case I already warned her that I probably wouldn't be able to make it. What with your health and all, I couldn't—"

"But I *want* you to," he replied. "The Franklins can look after me. In any case, do you think your old uncle is so selfish he wants to see you tied down all the time to an invalid?" It was clear he really meant what he said. It mattered a great deal to him that she attend, escorted by Syd Schaeffer.

"Well, we'll see," she replied. To herself she vowed not to go at all if it meant doing so with Syd. Somehow between now and then she'd squirm out of it.

"Nonsense!" cried the old man, shaking his head. "You'll go and have a good time the way pretty young girls are meant to do, and that's final. I'll not have you moping around here Saturday night. In fact, I forbid it!"

The abrupt nod of his head terminated all further discussion. Inwardly, secretly, Cathy prayed for more horrible weather.

After dinner she found herself alone with Syd in the parlor. Her uncle, pleading weariness, but with a calculating gleam in his eyes, had gone upstairs to bed again. Cathy resented being put in such a position. She knew her uncle had left them by themselves on purpose, hoping in his quaintly old-fashioned way that "romance would flower." Only Syd's good manners saved what would have otherwise have been a very irritating situation. At least Syd, though dull, was not the kind to inflict unwanted wrestling matches upon her. It made it easier to be gracious to him whose only fault, after all, was that he wasn't the one she desired.

Once they settled on the sofa, Syd suddenly turned to her. "Cathy, I have a surprise for you."

"A surprise?" In spite of herself her voice trembled. Crankily she reflected that she didn't want any surprises. She couldn't think of anything coming from him that she'd welcome, so she stared as he pulled from his inside jacket pocket a slim black leatherette box about six inches long. Her eyes widened in dismay as she watched him open it. Nestling in midnight-blue velvet glittered a delicate bracelet of white gold set with diamonds and emeralds.

"For you, Cathy." At once he reached to fasten it around her wrist.

Cathy jerked her hand away. "I couldn't!" she gasped. She stared at it in horror. From Derek, she could have accepted such a gift, but not from a man for whom she had no feelings. Flowers or some little trinket should have been all he offered. Suddenly she seemed to feel invisible hands grabbing at her, pulling her down into a morass of sticky entanglements where she didn't want to be.

"You can, and you *will*," he retorted with unusual firmness.

"No, Syd, please. It wouldn't be right." Such a gift implied obligation. Though the bracelet was beautiful, and just the sort of thing she'd have picked out for herself, she didn't want to owe Syd anything, not love, not even gratitude, and certainly not whatever else he might expect this luscious little bauble to buy. She glanced at him warily. "Syd, I appreciate the thought, really I do, but you'll have to take it back. I can't accept it. It's far too expensive and grand."

"I can't take it back," he replied, looking smug. "You'll just have to to keep it."

"Syd, *really*! I simply cannot. You shouldn't have bought this for me." She meant that with all her heart and soul. Truly she wished he hadn't.

But he had, and seemed determined that she relent. "Yes, I *should* have, and it's yours now and that's final."

"Syd!" She tried again. Now that her uncle had gone to bed, she felt freer to speak the truth. "I won't take it. I've been back in Malawi just a few days; we scarcely know each other after all these years. And even if we did . . . Well, this bracelet—" She shook her head. "It's simply too, too, expensive. Too major a gift."

"But I *want* you to have it." Persisting, his soft eyes pleaded with her. "Try to understand, its cost doesn't mean as much to me as it does to you. I think you're afraid it's a bribe with strings attached, but it's *not*, really it's not. It's a gift that I'll take pleasure just in giving. The green of those emeralds matches your eyes and it delights me to think of you wearing it."

"Syd, if I took it, I'd feel funny about it, and I don't want to. I'm sorry, but you'll have to take it back."

"No! I won't listen to this, Cathy. I won't take no for an answer. I laid eyes on this bracelet and I felt it already belonged to you . . . something beautiful to accent your loveliness and my greatest reward will be the sheer delight of seeing you wear it. I *refuse* to let you rob me of this one small pleasure just because of a few silly scruples. You'll keep the bracelet and that's that!"

Cathy blinked, surprised by the intensity of his outburst. "Well, really, I—I don't know what to say." His explosion had taken her completely aback while the pleading in his soft eyes touched her heart.

Self-doubts assailed her. How different he was from Derek. Derek, who could be so impossible, raised her senses to a pitch of aliveness not known since that long-lost summer of their youth. Poor Syd! She felt such a pang of pity for him. He was trying so hard to win her, to soften her heart, but he was going about it in all the wrong way. Or maybe there was no right way to win her from Derek. She knew now, beyond doubt, that she belonged with Derek, and not to any other man.

In the end she accepted Syd's bracelet, though reluctantly and with misgivings in her heart. When it came time for him to leave, Cathy walked with him to the door. "I'll see you Saturday," he said, kissing her lightly upon the lips.

Cathy stared at him in dismay. In the argument over accepting the bracelet, she had forgotten all about Saturday night. She glanced at him now with a fleeting frown. "About Saturday night," she began. "Let me get in touch with you on that." She wanted a chance to think things out and formulate, if necessary, an acceptable excuse for not going with him.

"Sure. But you'll wear your bracelet, won't you?"

He spoke this last pleadingly. His eyes mirrored his hopes. She heard those same feelings revealed in his voice and felt a pang of guilt.

The little bracelet hung like a cold weight against her slender wrist. It glittered in bright contrast to her suntanned skin. He had commented joyfully on how right he had been. The emeralds picked up the color and sparkle in her eyes, and in spite of herself Cathy's heart fluttered a little as she looked at it. After all, what woman does not love fine jewelry?

Cathy expected Derek to call the next day, but by midafternoon he still had not. Mrs. Franklin needed her to drive into Greenbrae, a nearby village, to pick up some staples at the local store. Cathy had gone, but only after getting Mrs. Franklin to promise that she or her husband would answer the phone whenever it rang, instead of letting her uncle do it, and that they'd relay to her any message.

But she discovered all too soon that her precautions with the phone were unnecessary. She learned to her dismay one very good reason why Derek had not yet called.

She had stopped for a solitary lunch at a combination inn and pub that served as the little settlement's only restaurant. It smelled of beer. Its cool humidity felt good when the weather was hot, but forbidding in the coolest days of the rainy season. Then only the fire crackling in its large open-pit fireplace welcomed one to the restaurant. As Cathy sat at her tiny table eating fish and chips and sipping the beer served warm, English-style, to which she had added two ice cubes, she heard snatches of gossip from people sitting at nearby tables. Suddenly she stiffened as she listened in on a few words exchanged by two older women nearby. Their chatter made her very hair rise.

"They say he wanted to wed her in Johannesburg but decided to wait." The voice came out in the smug, confidential tone so typical of a devoted gossip.

"They'll do it here, no doubt." Cathy looked back and saw the second nod in a knowing way.

"Aye, and with old man Van Ness throwin' the bash, it'll be a fine wedding indeed." The first woman sighed with barely suppressed envy.

"Ach, there she is now." The one sitting nearest to Cathy said, then stiffened to eager attention.

As both women at the neighboring table turned to gaze toward the one they were obviously gossiping about, Cathy followed their eyes with her own to catch a glimpse of a tall, blond woman sweeping in. The blonde stood warily at first, like a tigress scrutinizing surrounding countryside for danger. Her cold eyes darted around with a hard and intent expression as they tried to pierce the dimness inside that pub. The watchful look on her face, and even the subtle but unmistakable tension in her forward-leaning posture revealed she was searching out someone. Cathy didn't understand why just then, but looking at the woman set her on edge with wary defensiveness.

Cathy saw at once that the woman seemed out of place in this mostly rural part of the country. Her two-piece suit was too fashionable for backwoods Malawi, the heels of her beige leather boots were too high and stiletto-slender. Her makeup, dramatically applied, would have fitted well in a place like Johannesburg or New York City, but not here. Every short platinum curl seemed lacquered into place, and as Cathy looked at her, she felt instant dislike.

The intensity of her reaction surprised her at first. As the two gossiping women continued talking, Cathy began to understand why she felt as she did. It had been either telepathy or instinct . . . or that word "Johannesburg."

"Who would have thought it would be the Guenther man to win her," commented one in obvious wonderment. "Such a wild one he used to be."

"But wealthy now, or so they say," replied her companion. "He met her there, you know . . . in Johannesburg. Back here before, she wouldn't have given him the time of day."

"Aye, that's so," answered her friend, nodding.

By then Cathy's heart had plunged into a pit. Something that felt like a ball of molten lead burned in her stomach. Sudden nausea so overwhelmed her that she dropped the piece of fish she was holding. Suddenly she started and pulled back, hopefully out of sight. Derek himself had just entered.

From her little booth well in the shadows, she stared fascinated at the way his blue eyes glinted and flashed as they darted from side to side. With sinking heart, Cathy knew for whom he searched. She saw how his eyes fastened on the woman already identified by one of the gossips as Mina Van Ness. Their glance met, his and Mina's. Without smiling, with face strangely impassive, he nodded just slightly toward the doorway Cathy knew led to a smaller, more intimate area beyond the main room—a place where lovers nestled and businessmen concluded private transactions. They reached the doorway and without glancing around disappeared together into the shadows beyond.

chapter 10

SO THAT WAS why he hadn't called! He had been so busy with his Johannesburg fiancée he hadn't had time to bother. Maybe for a while he had succumbed to old memories of tenderness, and of course good old-fashioned red-blooded lust, but the moment his elegant Johannesburg fiancée blew into town it was "Goodbye, Cathy!" It all made such perfect, horrible sense.

Unable to remain where she was a moment longer, Cathy stood. On legs barely able to support her weight, she abandoned her half-eaten meal and managed to pay her bill at the cashier's stand. She stifled an urge to sob. Incredible dizziness washed over her. She was sure she was going to faint. Almost at once, however, angry pride asserted itself. She realized how Derek had led her on, toying with her emotions—and her body! No matter what agony he had put her through, she would not let him know how his deceit had made her suffer. She was too proud a woman to tolerate *that*, not a second time.

She had planned to back out of going with Syd to Mrs. Windon's party. She knew now she'd go through with it, flaunting Syd for all the world to see and comment on. After all, he, too, was rich, successful, good looking. He'd be considered quite a catch to all those gossips she'd met. Flushing with anger, she leaped into her car, the small city vehicle her uncle had bought for trips into Blantyre. Cursing herself for falling for Derek a second time, she roared back along the road to Tanyasi, unmindful of the tears searing her eyes.

With trembling hand she called Syd at work. Fighting to keep calm, she plunged right in. "The reason I told you I'd let you know about Saturday is that I wanted to decide on a good time to make our appearance. How about nine, Syd, with you picking me up at eight?" Syd couldn't see how Cathy's eyes flashed fire, and it was just as well. Derek couldn't do what he did to her! He had no right. She wouldn't stand for it. No way would she let him know how he had hurt her. She'd go and have the greatest time of her life at that party...with Syd.

"That sounds wonderful!" Syd cried happily. "I'll be there on the dot!"

Derek called that evening. She seethed in anger, but was determined to remain aloof and not reveal the extent of her pain. She felt she gave him every chance to explain, to volunteer the information that an old fiancée he had once loved but now discarded had come to visit. She had been willing to believe almost any explanation he gave, and after hinting, listened eagerly with rapidly sinking heart to the way he explained away his neglect of the past two days by pleading exhaustion and extreme business.

You were busy all right, she thought bitterly, busy with Mina Van Ness and she wore you out. Something deep inside rose to challenge her suspicion. Mina Van Ness was an ice maiden. It seemed unlikely that she'd have drummed up enough passion to wear *anyone* out... but then one never could tell!

Cathy dressed early. She was determined to look wonderful, if for no other reason than to spite Derek. She decided to wear her favorite gown, a cheongsam of bright green silk that matched her eyes. Its oriental style was becoming with arm openings slashed inward toward its mandarin-style collar to reveal the smooth, slender curves of her shoulders and upper arms. The narrow skirt hung around her ankles. Slashes on each side, reaching almost to her thigh, allowed her to walk comfortably as well as giving her, when she wore it, an extremely sophisticated appearance. It was a stunning gown that accented her exotic beauty and she loved it. Even better, this gown, more than any of her others, would go perfectly with Syd's bracelet. She intended to flash it and to make clear to anyone who asked that the man who had brought her to the party had given it to her. Blinking back the sudden rush of tears that threatened to ruin her eye makeup, Cathy vowed she'd let Derek see how little his callous, fickle indifference mattered to her.

After looking in one last time on her uncle, Cathy hurried downstairs. She greeted Syd calmly, then in a defiant, yet oddly jubilant mood accompanied him to the party where they found the festivities already in full swing. Mrs. Windon blinked with surprise to see Syd with Cathy instead of Cathy alone, a ready and willing partner, she believed, for Derek. Nevertheless she welcomed him graciously, then led them both into the main room. Candles burned in rich-looking chandeliers. At its far end near slender twin windows stood a banquet table covered with white damask. Upon it, there were plates of delicious-looking food and a huge cut-crystal punchbowl filled with red liquid.

Music issued from a stereo. Its rhythms and melodies mingled with the laughter and conversation of a crowd enjoying a party. Sound rippled back and forth, rising and falling. With heart pounding, Cathy glanced around. Most of the people were strangers. A few looked vaguely familiar. Some she knew from her last time in Malawi. Her eyes, however, darted past them all. She searched instead for Derek or any sign of his presence. More than anything she wanted to make sure he saw her with Syd.

Then she caught a glimpse of him. He stood off in

one corner with his back to her talking with some people. He didn't know yet that she had arrived. With a great surge of hope Cathy saw that he appeared to have come alone, circulating among Mrs. Windon's guests like any other unattached vistor.

Obviously the gossip had been wrong. She had misread the signs. She regretted not confronting him directly over the phone when he called, instead of hinting around, then waiting for him to practically read her mind and explain the whole thing away. A lot of misunderstandings would have cleared themselves up, but she hadn't come right out and asked and now she regretted it. She wished fervently she hadn't come with Syd. At once she scolded herself. Derek had waited three days before he called. Why should she stay at home only to come running after him lika faithful dog whenever he whistled. To hell with it! Even if all the gossip and the evidence of her own eyes proved false, she wasn't about to let him take her for granted.

However, uneasiness remained. Uncomfortable now, but trying to ignore it, she circulated around with Syd, allowing him to introduce them both to other guests. They made the usual sorts of small talk typical of such gatherings, and Cathy found it dull. From time to time she glanced toward Derek who had as yet not noticed her.

chapter 11

HE DID NOT come to her. He stared, face taut and the sinews of his jaw cordlike from hard-clenched teeth. Suddenly, without changing expression, he turned away, his back to her. Cathy fumed. Finding herself the target of such rudeness, yet at the same time guiltily understanding the reason why, she knew now she had made a mistake bringing Syd here. Whatever lay between her and Derek, good and bad, would not be helped by arousing his anger or jealousy.

She reached for the cup of punch Syd had poured. Her hand trembled. Rather than risk staining her favorite gown from a bad spill, she quickly set her drink

back down. Forcing herself to be poised, she smiled
at everybody, yet nobody in particular, then turned
around. Syd had begun talking with a banker from
Blantyre. Cathy joined in the conversation, pretending
far more enthusiasm than she actually felt. Jellylike
inside, she tried to ignore Derek's presence.

After a few minutes had passed and she believed
she was calmer, she raised her punch cup to her lips
again. Somehow she had expected just ordinary fruit
punch. As she got a whiff of it, however, she blinked
with surprise at the smell of strong rum. The party had
taken on a certain good-natured loudness. Now that
she had drunk some of that punch, she understood
why. It was *too* strong. When she sensed a presence
moving toward her from behind, she whirled uneasily,
thinking it might be Derek. It wasn't and when she
saw who really approached, Cathy felt grateful that
she had braced herself.

This particular evening Mina Van Ness looked very
sleek indeed with her shiny white-blond hair swept
upward from her face. Its very style gave her an incredibly polished appearance. She had applied her
makeup heavily but artfully. Cathy disliked everything
about it, just as she already detested the woman herself. Cathy would have given anything to avoid meeting her, but the woman obviously felt otherwise, and
since it was Cathy whom she zeroed in on with eyes
fixed, and not someone else, she knew she was
trapped. The hostility in Mina Van Ness's cold blue
eyes was scarcely veiled.

"So *you're* Cathy!" Her lips twisted in a faintly

scornful smile as her eyes raked Cathy up and down with an ill-concealed contempt. "I've heard so much about you lately...from so many people." She went on in a purringly sarcastic tone. "Gossip *does* travel, doesn't it!"

"And *you* must be Mina." Cathy vowed she'd show up the woman by remaining airily pleasant. She'd not give her antagonist the satisfaction of seeing how angry and uneasy she had become. "And I've heard so much about you too." Let her wonder, Cathy thought with a certain nasty satisfaction. To her delight the woman's gaze flickered for just an instant with uncertainty. However, she recovered her poise almost immediately.

"Yes, well it shouldn't surprise me that you had," she replied. "My family has been here for generations."

From the way she subtly accented certain words, Cathy knew Mina sneered at her uncle who had bought Tanyasi relatively recently by local standards.

"Mina, dear, how did you like Johannesburg?" a woman standing nearby asked.

"I *loved* it, of course," Mina replied. She tossed her head. "It has life, excitement..."

"Don't you ever miss your home?" asked one of the others. "After all, you grew up in Malawi."

Mina shrugged. "It's a pretty enough place, but *really!*" Her lips parted.

To Cathy, the woman's small, quick grimace of distaste was obvious. No one else seemed to notice, however, how deeply this sleek polished woman despised the countryside. If they did, they pretended not to. Cathy knew Mina might tolerate living in Blantyre, but she belonged in Johannesburg or some other large, important city and she knew it. Worst of all she seemed to despise anyone who preferred to live otherwise. A woman like Mina Van Ness would never be content with anything less, and if she ever succeeded in dragging Derek to the altar, she'd probably force him into her life-style, far away from the land he loved.

Cathy chewed her lip. She would never make such awful demands on Derek, no woman would do that to a man she really loved. Cathy felt a surge of anger at Derek. If he chose Mina, then he deserved whatever life his not-so-blushing-bride would inflict on him. She glanced in his direction. To her dismay their eyes met . . . and she knew an odd mix of emotions—pity, anger, yearning. It was disturbing, painful. She turned away quickly. Why, why, she asked herself, did Derek allow himself to become involved with Mina? It was, strangely, as though he insulted her by taking up with a woman like that.

"Can we ever hope that you'll be back to stay, Mina?" a man asked.

Mina gave another little toss of her well-coiffed head. "Well, I don't really know," she replied coyly. "It all depends."

No one else caught the malevolent look she flashed at Cathy. There was possessiveness in Mina's hard blue eyes—and another emotion she couldn't read.

"I have some attachments," the woman went on to explain, "most particularly attachments in Johannesburg. What I finally do, where I end up really depends on those attachments."

Cathy could stand Mina's company no longer, and excused herself, then rejoined Syd who had gone off on his own. The conversation he was having with two other businessmen bored her. Still, she preferred the friendly company to sparring with an unwanted adversary. Her mind wandered, only to be pulled sharply back to the present by a snatch of conversation that drifted to her ear.

"I hear she and Derek Guenther were lovers in Johannesburg," a woman Cathy didn't know whispered to another. Compelled to look, Cathy turned toward Mina. She saw that Derek had joined her, and the two were talking and laughing together. At that instant Derek glanced defiantly toward Cathy as if challenging her to do something about what she saw. His eyes narrowed and—so clear and vivid they reminded her of crystals—they flashed blue sparks at her. Sudden heat stole into Cathy's cheeks. She knew that before the evening ended, she'd come face to face with Derek Guenther in a fiery confrontation that would probably blister both of them.

"... engaged, weren't they?" she heard the woman's voice again.

"Maybe still are," replied the other. "With Mina you never know, though."

Cathy felt sick. On trembling legs she left the main room with its oppressive noisy party crowd. She meandered, searching for a place where she could have solitude until she recovered herself. She hoped Mrs. Windon wouldn't mind her wandering about, but there was nothing else she could do, not in her frame of mind.

She stepped into the deserted solarium filled with dripping ferns and exotic orchids. She found the atmosphere warm, perfumed, dimly aglow with indirect lighting—an attractive and comforting room. Her high heels clicked rapidly over the flagstone floor. The room appeared to be a favorite one for Mrs. Windon, its white-painted wicker furniture looked well used. All the place needed to complement its tropical-jungle atmosphere, Cathy thought, were a few birds flying free. A good room, a very good room, she decided, with a happy feeling to it.

She sank into a deep, softly cushioned armchair. Her fingers dug into her temples, and she shut her eyes. What was Derek—and her emotion for him—doing to her? She'd come to Malawi to work hard on the management of the wildlife reserve and to help care for her uncle. Or had she fooled herself—and really come here more to find Derek again than to discharge her family responsibilities. She was so obsessed by Derek that her duty scarcely could crowd into her thoughts. Madness. Her love for Derek was sheer madness, reducing her to nothing more than a quivering mass of emotions. She heard soft footsteps on the flagstone behind her. She dropped her hands into her lap and turned to the sound.

"What do you want?" she gasped.

"To talk to you," Derek growled. A vein pulsed in his temple. His face had flushed a deep, angry scarlet.

"There's nothing really to say," she retorted, stepping back. Her lashes flickered as she glanced around.

"There's *everything* to say," he came back at her.

"For starters, what made you think you had the right to bring along an uninvited guest to my aunt's party?"

Cathy's eyes widened. "Your aunt?"

"Yes, my aunt! And my dearest friend as well. What right had you to bring that man here? She invited *you*, not a crowd."

"One additional person hardly constitutes a crowd, Derek. Anyway, she didn't mind."

"She's far too gracious to show it if she did," he retorted.

"This isn't a dinner party, for heaven's sake, it's an open house. In any case, I doubt if it's my 'uninvited' guest who bothers you so much."

"Cathy, you're right. I wouldn't give a damn if you showed up with an entire soccer team!"

Cathy shrugged. "I notice you didn't come here alone tonight either."

"So that's it! Well, whatever you've heard about me and Mina—"

"You know, Derek, the two of you make a perfect couple. She's a barracuda and you're a shark." The cold anger went out of her. "After all we shared. Why, Derek?"

He looked enraged . . . and terrifying, yet he spoke in a low voice. "Maybe I decided on self-preservation instead of lust."

"What do you mean?"

"I am a man of the country, my dear Cathy, and I've learned the lesson nature has to teach those of us who are to learn."

"What has nature to do with this?"

"The old, old story of the female spider, Cathy. That's what you remind me of, you know. You can't trust, apparently, and so you can't be trusted."

"Oh, no? That's really the pot calling the kettle," she said icily. "There are any number of people who'd be not only willing, but glad to give a character reference quite contrary to the one you hurl out so irresponsibly."

"Someone like that weak-chinned fool you came with tonight?"

She ground her teeth in anger. "He cares, Derek. More than you ever did or could." On impulse her arm shot out. She held it ramrod stiff in front of him with fist clenched so that he could see the diamond and emerald bracelet glittering upon her wrist. The beautiful earth-hardened fires of the gems leaped to flame under the electric light. She was thrilled that another man cared enough about her to have offered her such a gift. She was delighted she could use it against Derek.

"So *that's* what you want!" His brows raised. Scorn replaced the anger in his eyes. "If it's expensive gifts that turn you on, I can buy you all the diamonds in Johannesburg!"

"Save them for Mina, Derek!" She whirled away, but he caught her. His powerful hands yanked her back, then spun her around so that she was forced to look at him. Angrily she struggled to jerk away. "I wouldn't take the Hope diamond itself from the likes of *you*!"

"I doubt *that*!" His quiet voice cut into her like a

knife. "If I brought you the Hope diamond, you'd probably fall onto your back in a minute."

Cathy's eyes flew open. "How dare you!" she gasped and flung the palm of her hand hard against his face with a resounding slap.

"Why you . . . !" With a swift move he grabbed her wrist. The pressure of his fingers made the bracelet cut into her skin.

Derek held her for what seemed an eternity, just looking at her. Finally he said in a voice of deadly calm. "Some men hit back."

But he did not. Raking her with a contemptuous look one final time, he lowered her wrist. He turned on his heels and left. She gulped a deep, steadying breath and with cold determination rejoined the party. Once back in circulation she made a point of proving to everyone, but especially to Derek, that his arrogance mattered so little to her that she could still have a good time. She flirted a bit, smiling and laughing. She felt particularly grateful to Syd and found his presence reassuring. As they danced, his arms became a haven from the storm Derek had created in her heart.

They were talking when someone put on a rollicking, rather corny polka. At once Syd, a little loosened by the punch, suggested they join in. She moved with him out onto the dance floor, created when someone cleared away the furniture. Along with about six other couples, they bounced in rhythm to the polka. Cathy felt a little silly, but she had to admit that in spite of herself she was having a good time doing this dance. Finally the accordion wheezed down as with a sigh of relief. Flushed and breathless she and Syd clung to one another, recovering. She laughed a little awkwardly, then glanced again under lowered lashes to where Derek stood glowering at her from across the room.

She turned away from his eyes fixed upon her with such hard intensity. But there was no escape from him and the turmoil he created in her.

Waltz music played and Syd pulled her into his arms. As the music swelled, growing louder, its graceful rhythm attracted more and more dancers until about twenty couples dipped and spun through the room.

"I'm having a really good time, Cathy!" Syd murmured into her ear. "Let's plan to go dancing often."

"Yes," she replied. Silently she added that she'd make sure the next time Derek Guenther was not standing so close by. Midway through the next dance, another waltz, a shadow fell across them.

"Mind if I cut in?" The question was actually a command, uttered with smooth but forceful intensity. Cathy's heart sank. Why didn't Derek just leave her alone?

Syd's brows raised in surprise, but he answered smoothly, "Certainly. You have good taste." He nodded to Cathy, smiling, then stepped away so that Derek could take his place. Cathy's heart plunged. The glitter in Derek's eyes was as cold as the skillfully faceted rocks set into the bracelet she wore around her wrist.

"So that's your new hearthrob, Cathy?"

"He's a *friend*, Derek, and that's all I care to say."

"If that's *all* he is, then you've got some explaining to do to *him*," Derek said. "He's not looking at you like a friend."

"That's *my* problem, isn't it." Defiantly Cathy forced herself to glare back into his eyes.

His jaw hardened. "You seem to take great delight, don't you, in playing games with people, or maybe it's just you enjoy the gifts they give you."

"What gives *you* the right to be so damned self-righteous? Your friend over there," she added, nodding to where Mina stood watching them, "seems as sure as everyone else that you plan to marry her. It makes me wonder about *you*, Derek, and your honesty."

"I never lied to Mina about my intentions," he retorted. Luckily the din of music and voices muffled the scene they otherwise would have been making.

"I never lied to Syd about mine," she retorted, "so I really wonder just what your intentions toward Mina are. I won't ask about *me*—where *I* stand in all this mess. You've made it all too clear on *that* score."

His eyes flashed. "Damn it, Cathy, you're impossible."

"You sound as though you think you own me. Well, you don't, and you won't."

"I never want to own you," he retorted, "only to possess you."

"Go to the devil!" Bright color flushed her skin. The music slowed to a stop. Cathy tried to push away from him, furious for the way he had treated her during that dance, but he held her and would not let go. "My uncle was right about you, Derek Guenther," she whispered, furious. "You're a swine. Always were and always will be."

His eyes glittered in cold amusement mingled with a look of strange determination that alarmed her. Suddenly, before she realized what he was about to do, and certainly before she could have done anything to stop him, his head swooped down. He smashed a hard and angry kiss on her mouth. His hands ran harshly, insulting over her back and down to her hips for everyone in the room to see.

chapter 12

HOW LONG HE held her in that embrace she would never know. It seemed forever. She sensed every pair of eyes was on them, alone in the center of the room, locked in a kiss that made a mockery of passion. She had struggled to no avail, now suddenly a swift, hard push set her free. She turned from Derek and without a word walked slowly away.

The music started up again. Guests tried to pick up the threads of conversation as if nothing had happened.

Determined that no one would see how deeply the incident had upset her, she fixed her face into an expression of masklike hardness. Staring straight ahead with chin high, she made her way to the nearest door. Gaining the hallway, she went straight to the heavy wooden front door. She heard footsteps, but did not stop or turn. Her one goal was to reach the door and the night beyond it.

"Cathy, I'm sorry!" Mrs. Windon's voice was agitated, genuinely regretful. "I never dreamed my nephew would dare to embarrass you or anyone else as he just did. I do apologize, dear. He must be out of his senses. Too much punch?"

Cathy shook her head, closing her eyes briefly and sighing wearily. "No," she said softly, "not too much to drink. That was a form of revenge on Derek's part."

"Revenge?"

"Derek and I seem to have a rather awful effect on one another. I'm afraid that together we act like temperamental, unruly children. Neither of us behaves with the least maturity or judgment."

Mrs. Windon's eyes held sympathy, but a kind of soft amusement, too. "All fireworks and raw emotion, eh? And not the least bit of sense between you two. Is that it?"

"Something like that. I'm not sure I really understand anything beyond the fact that Derek and I are not right for each other. We can't seem to communicate—only argue or . . ." Cathy's voice trailed off.

"Or make love?" Mrs. Windon supplied.

Cathy shrugged, reluctant to confide any more. "Hopeless. Both of us."

"Cathy, Cathy," Syd called, rushing toward her along the hallway. "My dear, how awful for you."

"She'll survive," Mrs. Windon said tartly. Obviously Syd was not her favorite guest. She handed Cathy her wrap. "Don't worry about this little incident. A mere tempest in a teapot and it won't make much of a stir. I'll put it 'round that my nephew was overcome by the rum and that I shan't be serving this particular punch again in the near future." She chuckled, then hugged Cathy warmly. "Trust me, it won't damage the life you'll be trying to build here."

"Thank you," Cathy murmured and returned the hug. She gathered her wrap around her shoulders and left, Syd trailing her. Once outside, he stopped and put his arms around her.

"He's the one who looked bad, honey," Syd said, "not you."

"Stop it," she commanded him gently. She didn't want Syd's pity, anyone's pity.

"Why did he do it? What's between you two anyway?"

Reasonable enough, Cathy thought. Questions anyone might ask and that probably a number of people at the party *were* asking at this very moment. "Derek and I used to be very close when we were both much younger... but it was a mistake... *a terrible mistake!*"

"I guess so—if tonight was any indication." After a pause he glanced at her. "Do you still love him?"

"Love him?" Cathy burst into a short, shrill laugh. "Right now I could murder him! Syd, what you saw, what everyone in there saw were a lot of leftover emotions running around with no place to go."

"So it's all over between you two?" Syd glanced hopefully at her.

Cathy exhaled sharply. "I'm not a masochist, Syd." She walked toward the car. As he opened the door for her, she put a detaining hand on his arm. "I'd be grateful if you wouldn't mention this to Uncle Howard. The . . . the subject of Derek Guenther upsets him."

"Of course not," Syd agreed readily, but there was a questioning look in his eyes.

They were silent on the ride home. Back at Africa House, Syd wordlessly led her to the door and very gently kissed her good night.

Howard's condition was growing worse. The dismal changes that had taken place in the short time since her return to Malawi, to Africa House, were all too apparent to Cathy. She'd been hard hit by his appearance when she'd stopped in to see him early this morning. His coloring had altered, deepening to an ashen hue, his breathing was more labored. His face was scored with harsh lines of pain . . . and weariness of that pain. In stark contrast to the reality of her uncle's present condition, Cathy was flooded with images of the Howard she'd known and loved in her childhood and early womanhood. Time and time again she saw the physically powerful man, recalled episodes showing his strong, enthusiastic, optimistic, domineering personality.

Cathy was closeted in the little office on the ground floor of Africa House trying to order the confusion of invoices, correspondence, receipts, and odd pieces of papers with near indecipherable scribbles that littered the polished mahogany surface. Her thoughts were only partly fixed on the task; they moved freely between the events at the party, Derek and the sickroom above. One or both of the Franklins were with her uncle trying to relieve his invalid's boredom with his pain and isolation. He was slipping away very fast now, Cathy realized, giving up more every day since her arrival. Perhaps he'd only hung on for her to reach him so that he could ease out of life secure in the knowledge of her guardianship of his beloved Tanyasi acres.

The reserve held back the encroaching civilization that would destroy precious species of animals now rare except in the zoos of the world. And it was a haven, too, for some of the Nyanja tribesmen who didn't want to give up the old ways and found "work" on the reserve compatible with their traditions and beliefs. Tanyasi had been what her uncle had lived for the last twenty or twenty-five years. Tanyasi... and her. She had no doubts after the last days that she had been the substitute for the child he had never sired.

And this house, she reflected, this marvelous, rambling old Victorian mansion, Africa House, how much it meant, too. Its dual functions seemed at odds sometimes to Cathy. It was "command center" for the battle to save animals from the pressures of population and it was a cushioned, comfortable respite from the struggles of the world. She realized with reluctance that all this was soon to be hers.

Far off, she heard the ringing of the telephone. She

had disconnected the bell on the instrument on the desk first thing this morning and left word with the Franklins that she wouldn't take calls. She neither wanted to talk with the curious, posing as friendly new acquaintances, nor with people she'd known in the past. The latter, of course, included Derek, if he tried to call—and that was a big if. She had spent a sleepless night, pacing and thinking. There was a hard knot of pained resolve in her as a result. She and Derek, still physically attracted to one another, had lost all the friendship, the warm feelings of real and deep caring for one another because of the misunderstanding surrounding their parting after the accident. Now they'd both grown up...and changed. There was a ruthlessness in Derek that hadn't been there before. And in her. There was a need for a true, lasting close relationship built on shared values. She and Derek were no good for one another...basically not in sympathy.

There was a brief knock and the door swung open. Mrs. Franklin entered, a heaviness to her step and a slump in her posture that signalled Cathy all too well as to her uncle's worsening condition. She frowned. "Does he need me now?" she asked.

"Not directly, Cathy, dear. I mean he needs you to do what you're doing, keep Tanyasi going. But he doesn't need you to be with him at the moment. Nor me either. He's in pain just now. I think he's more easy with showing it when Mr. F. is at his side."

Cathy nodded. "You and I are a strain on him. He tries so darned hard to put up a good show for us."

"Too proud," Mrs. Franklin agreed. She sighed heavily, then straightened her shoulders. "Well, now," she said briskly, pulling a paper from the pocket of her housedress. "Here's the list of odds and ends we'll need. I'd send Raymond or someone else, but there's your uncle's medicine to be got with the changed prescriptions and a few other things to tend to in Blantyre that I think you must do."

"Don't sound so apologetic, please," Cathy said firmly. "I can pick up on this desk work later. Tonight even. Besides, I've an important personal matter to take care of in town anyway."

"Not..." Mrs. Franklin's voice was overloud on that one word and then it settled to a near whisper. "He's been calling, you know. Almost on the hour every hour."

Cathy took a deep breath. Her eyes strayed to the window and an unfixed point beyond. "I know. I intend to deal with Derek soon, but not just yet, Mrs. Franklin." Her gaze swung back to the woman. "The list?" She walked toward the motherly figure and took the paper. "I... probably will make it back in time for supper, but don't worry about me if I'm late."

She brushed past Mrs. Franklin, giving her an affectionate pat on the shoulder, then hurrying away. She went straight to her room and changed from jeans to a trim green and white plaid dress with jacket. She slipped on black patent-leather sandals and transferred items into a shiny and very roomy black handbag. The day was diamond-bright and she picked up her large sunglasses to ease the glare during the long drive ahead. She took a box from her dresser drawer and eased it into the zip compartment of her bag, shaking her head ruefully as she did so.

Down the hall she steeled herself at the closed door to her uncle's bedroom. Assuming a bright smile, she knocked softly and entered.

"I'm off to Blantyre," she said breezily, "off to do all those errands you've piled up for me, slave driver." She hated the false note of cheer she'd struck. And from the look on her uncle's face he was neither fooled, nor pleased either.

"Come closer, Cathy. That's good. I want you to get back on the early side and make a special point to come in and talk with me tonight. Understood?"

She frowned, started to react to the ominous tone in his voice, but thought better of it and merely commented, "I wouldn't miss a conversation with you for the world. So I won't dally with the shopping." She gave him a farewell peck on the cheek, said good-bye to Mr. Franklin, and left the room in a hurry. Her heart was heavy with sadness . . . and with a kind of foreboding, not only about her uncle's deteriorated condition, but about that "talk" he wanted to have this evening.

One of her uncle's employees had already gone out and brought back the Land-Rover. She passed it in the garage where it rested on blocks while Raymond, their prize mechanic, worked to rebuild its shattered engine. Fortunately her uncle owned a second Land-Rover. In addition, he had a small car which he used for touring. It was the best vehicle to take into Blantyre. She went to it and slipped behind the wheel. A faint smile touched her lips. Derek. She hoped he wasn't right about her being a jinx where anything mechanical was concerned! The last thing she needed was another accident or breakdown. Her smile started to sour, but quickly reasserted itself. She had to keep her personal sorrow about her relationship with Derek out of her mind. She had to maintain her hard-gained perspective, her awareness of her own maturity, particularly in light of what she faced—with dread—in the near future with her uncle.

As she approached the outer boundaries of the reserve and saw the outlying farms ahead, she felt a renewed pang of love for the beauty of Tanyasi. How precious, how special it was in a land almost totally changed by the generations of settlers who had tilled its rolling hills into fields and driven away its wildlife.

Its grandeur of preserved wilderness affected her with ever-fresh intensity. She knew she belonged here. She always had. The blood of Tanyasi flowed in her veins. It beat through her heart and she turned to it now for comfort, grateful that her uncle had summoned her back. Thank God it wasn't going to be up for sale to be turned into yet another farm! No matter what happened in her private life, she was determined to keep Tanyasi as she and her uncle wanted it to be. She would stay in Malawi—Derek Guenther notwithstanding. And she would build a good and purposeful life for herself here.

She knew where she had to start, too. She had to rectify a dreadful mistake. And so the first place she headed for in Blantyre was Syd's office. The bracelet he'd given her was a heavy weight in her handbag, a worse weight on her conscience. Not only had she been every kind of a fool in flaunting it to Derek, she'd been a miserable person to allow Syd to push it at her in the first place.

Luckily she found a parking space not too far from Syd's office building. She was anxious to get this task over and virtually ran along the sidewalk to the chrome-trimmed glass doors and up the stairs to his second-floor suite. She remembered this place all too well from her childhood forays into Blantyre and from Syd's tireless description of the office building he'd personally restored and redecorated. She felt sad for him, since he considered this one of the major achievements of his career.

A receptionist blinked through thick-lensed glasses as Cathy inquired about seeing "Mr. Shaeffer." She was both disconcerted and relieved to learn he was in Johannesburg on business.

"Is there anything *I* could do?" the receptionist asked.

"Y-Yes, as a matter of fact you *could*. I want to leave something for him, along with a confidential message. The . . . the item I have to leave is very valuable. Do you have a safe here?"

"Yes we do. I can put it in for you and I'll put you at Mr. Shaeffer's desk to write your note," the woman said, rising and leading Cathy into a comfortable room with dark red leather upholstery and an impressive oriental rug on the floor. The woman made a few pleasant comments and left Cathy alone. She took the box with the bracelet from her handbag and wrote a simple, straightforward message about its return. She sat back for a moment then and gazed out the windows set at angles and giving an interesting view of the busy streets outside. Unbidden came a question. Where was Derek's office in this concrete jungle, the office his aunt said he only tolerated, preferring to escape it to the simple life at his lodge? She sighed in exasperation at herself and rose quickly.

The formalities of placing the bracelet and note in the safe took only a few minutes and she was out on the streets of Blantyre again, off to do the numerous errands on Mrs. Franklin's list.

About ten minutes away from Africa House an ambulance passed her car. Soon after she saw another car coming toward her along the bitumenized road. An unusal amount of traffic she thought wryly. The sleek, glossy little sports car approaching at great speed seemed terribly out of place here in the countryside near the Shire River. Even in Blantyre a car of such delicacy was rarely seen. Skilled mechanics to service such cars were hard to find and parts for them were even harder to come by.

As the car passed her, roaring along the road, Cathy peered across to get a good look at the impractical soul driving it. And the sight made her clutch the steering wheel for dear life. His blond hair whipping in the wind, Derek looked dashingly handsome. His shirt

was open at the throat, exposing the medal he always
wore around his neck. That was all she had time to
glimpse—and the person who rode beside him. A
gauzy chiffon scarf held down carefully coiffed platinum hair. Mina, of course!

chapter **13**

HER UNCLE WAS waiting for her, propped by half a dozen pillows, looking worse than she had imagined he could look. Even the soft, rosy glow of the bedside lights did little to relieve the grim tones of his skin. How much weight he'd lost, she realized with a stab of pain. He looked so gaunt, so tortured resting against the harshly white pillowcases.

He smiled wanly at her and gestured to the chair pulled close to the side of the bed.

"We're going to have a late supper together," she told him, beaming down on him. "I heard you've eaten next to nothing today, and I've only just got back from

Blantyre. So I asked Mrs. Franklin to bring us a nice tray to share. How is that with you?"

"Fine, Cathy. Though I think you know I'm not much interested in food. It's talk I want. A nice, long air-clearing talk."

Curiously Cathy felt on edge. She knew her uncle was about to make some revelations, and it wasn't hard to figure out what they concerned. But she also knew she had to make it easy for him. "I'm not very hungry myself, Uncle Howard. So let's talk. We'll just put the tray aside when it comes, shall we?"

There was a trace of the amusement in his eyes that Cathy had known so many years growing up—along with the look of concern he'd so often displayed over her well-being.

"Don't patronize me, dear. It's hard enough being in this condition without everyone around reducing me to an infantile state. And no soft soap for this dirty situation, understand?"

"I understand." Cathy gulped. She sat down quickly to spare him the effort of looking up at her. Their eyes held one another for long seconds, then she looked away, wincing at the naked truth of the nearness of his death which she had heard in his words and then read in his face.

"That's better," he said, taking in her expression, silently acknowledging her new acceptance of what he had long accepted. "I believe you can guess what I want . . . no, need . . . to talk about."

"Derek," she said emphatically, but in a hushed tone.

His gaze shifted uneasily. "The Guenther family, actually," he corrected.

There was a long silence between them, the hum of the electric generator outside and the ticking clock within breaking the wordless vacuum in the room.

When he finally did speak, Cathy was startled by the sound of his voice.

"You didn't have to tell me who it was who rescued you that day when the Land-Rover gave out. No need to mention where you spent that night. I knew right away just taking one look at you, Cathy."

"Uncle Howard," she whispered, "I'm a grown woman with desires, needs."

"I know." His firm tone surprised her. "You matured early—perhaps too early—and it always worried me."

He grimaced, but Cathy couldn't be certain whether from pain or emotion over the subject.

"From the point of view of the Guenther family, Cathy, there is every reason to hate me and mine. Frankly I don't blame anyone of them. I'd probably feel the same, in their shoes." With a sigh he went on to explain how years ago he had been involved in business dealings with Derek's father.

"Pieter made mistakes. The fact that he drank and gambled was at the heart of it. I tried to warn him, but he was as pigheaded as anyone could be." Her uncle sighed. "Well, through no fault of mine he ended up losing everything, while I, not realizing to whom they had belonged, bought up some shares on the open market and gained controlling interest in three small local companies. Only later did I realize that Pieter's loss was my gain. But he believed I had arranged somehow to ruin him." The old man shook his head. "His mind was already going by then, I suppose because of the dissipated way of life he'd chosen."

"He couldn't blame you," Cathy protested.

"Oh, but he did." He waved a frail hand to ward off her further protests.

"There was more. Later on, about three years later to be exact, I began looking for a place in the country to settle. I had enough money by then to do exactly as I pleased and I had always dreamed of something like Tanyasi. I checked with local real estate agents and found a few promising parcels up for sale—and then this great big wonderful one. As it turned out," he said in a rush as if he wanted to get everything out as quickly as possible, "this very spot seemed best of all, and so I bought it." He took a long, gasping breath. "Doing so only reinforced Pieter's fanatical belief that I was out to ruin him in every way I could."

"I don't understand." Cathy leaned to him. "Why would he have thought such a thing?"

As he glanced at her, an odd expression flickered momentarily across his face. When he spoke again, however, his voice had recovered its calm. It sounded weaker though, and with sinking heart Cathy knew she'd have to leave him alone soon to rest. "I was living in Blantyre during my business years—traveling to Johannesburg but always returning to Blantyre and my flat there. I saw Pieter in Blantyre, not anywhere else, and I knew precious little about him except...well, except what I found out with increasing dismay about his personal life and weaknesses. I never knew, for instance, about his ancestral home. *I just never knew*."

"Uncle Howard, please," Cathy said forcefully, alarmed at the anguish he was experiencing. She stroked his hand. "There's no need to say more, not if talking about all this is going to affect you so."

He made a visible effort to regain his composure. "I must talk about it, Cathy. Otherwise how are you ever to understand . . . to go ahead with whatever you must." He gripped her hand fervently. "You must believe that I wouldn't have bought Tanyasi—and Africa House on it—never would have settled here if I had known. This land, this house, had all been in receivership. The bank held the papers in the bankruptcy proceeding. You see, all this that's mine and will be yours once belonged to the Guenther family."

Cathy's gasp of surprise quivered in the hushed room.

"It was the final straw for Pieter. He hated me then. He blamed me for the shambles he had made of his own life—and he did so with violent intensity. He passed all that along to his son, Derek. I never told you, or anyone, but I saw them in Blantyre one day when Derek was only about five years old. Already the child had been taught to hate." The old man frowned hard. "I won't go into it, Cathy, but he did. I never blamed the child."

It all began to make sense at last, Cathy realized in rather stunned wonder. She could feel her uncle's suspicions of Derek as clearly as if they were her own.

"You never disapproved of him because he was poor, did you? Nor because of his father? I can't— couldn't ever—see you as a man who would make the son suffer for the sins of the father! You believed, feared that Derek only wanted to get at you through me."

He nodded slowly. "And so I stepped in to prevent it. After the accident when he was trying to reach you, I drove him off, Cathy, told him you never wanted to see him again."

Now she could believe Derek's explanation about six years ago which had seemed so thin to her during his telling of it at his lodge.

"My God," Howard murmured, "I pray I didn't make a tragic mistake."

"No, no," Cathy assured him . . . and tried to assure herself as well. How would her life have been different with Derek in it? Had he been out for revenge or had he really loved her?

Something still bothered her, something she didn't understand. "Uncle Howard." She leaned close to him. "Why would Derek's father believe so strongly you wanted to get him? Surely there was some way you could have forced him to see the unfortunate chain of coincidences that occured."

"Derek's mother was a good woman, too good for Pieter," he said enigmatically. "As for Pieter, well, his mind went, that's all I can say."

There was more, much more to this story, Cathy realized, but her uncle was either unwilling or unable to go on with it now. His eyes closed. An expression of soul-deep weariness covered his face.

"Go now, Cathy," he murmured. His voice was barely audible. "I'm so tired. I need to rest."

"Yes, yes of course." With sinking heart she kissed his old cheek, then quietly padded out of the room. A strange sort of urgency gripped her. One taste of the truth and now she wanted, needed to drink deeply and fully of it. Her happiness depended on it. It was more than time that she and Derek faced one another, confronted their personal truths, and sorted out their past. Then, they would both be free to live in the present . . . and in the future.

chapter 14

THE CONFRONTATION WITH Derek turned out to be confrontation all right—but nothing like the one Cathy had anticipated earlier in the evening when she left her uncle's sickroom. She had intended to call Derek's office the next morning to arrange an appointment, but as she prepared for bed, there was a loud, persistent knock on the massive carved wooden front door. Mr. Franklin was with her uncle; Mrs. Franklin was taking a well-deserved rest in her apartment at the back of the house. Cathy snatched a robe and raced downstairs to answer the door before whoever was there roused the whole household.

Cathy flung open the door. "What is the meaning of..." Her words died in her throat. Syd, a very different Syd, stood with balled fist, ready to strike the door that was no longer in front of him. His face was red, his hair awry. Cathy did a stutter-step backward, away from the man she knew, yet didn't know.

"You...you returned the bracelet," Syd accused. "My secretary left a note telling me something had been put in the safe for me. I just got back from Johannesburg, tired, and to find...well, I was shocked to find it there. Shocked at your cold note."

Cathy took a deep breath and pulled the robe more tightly around her body. "Please come in, Syd. We can hardly discuss anything standing here in the doorway."

He pushed splayed fingers through his disheveled hair, then entered and followed Cathy through to the living room. She sat, but he paced.

"I thought we'd settled the matter of the bracelet. You accepted it, even wore it to the party. Do you intend to make a fool of me now?"

"Of course not, Syd," Cathy said with a deliberately low, calming voice. "I made a fool of *myself* accepting and wearing it—not a fool of you!"

He towered over her, raking her body with a hot look before staring hard into her eyes. "Cathy, from the first moment I laid eyes on you when you were a kid, then again when I picked you up at the airport, I've wanted you. Wanted you like a crazy man. Don't you know what that present was all about?"

"Perhaps I did," she murmured, her eyes falling to

her lap. "Perhaps that's exactly the reason I returned it. I'm not what you may think I am, even though I did, temporarily, accept such a valuable—"

"Stop it! I wasn't trying to buy your sweet favors with that bauble. And I don't want you just a few times as a mistress. I've got to have you to myself, for keeps, Cathy."

"I'm not a 'thing' to be owned," she shouted, then blanched. Wasn't that very much what she'd said to Derek?

Her uncle's words came back to her about her early physical development and the problems it presented. She realized suddenly that she'd never got over it. That she'd always held people at a distance, men especially, because her exceptional good looks made her wonder if she was liked for herself or only because she was a beautiful person. Her shoulders slumped.

"Syd, I'm a human being with feelings, dreams," she said in a very small voice. "I'm not a display item, not a prize to be shown off."

"Fool!" Syd spat out. "The only place I want to show you off is in my bed—and only to me!"

She inhaled sharply and jumped to her feet. "I'm not some kind of sex object either!"

He shouted back at her then and she was about to reply, but the sound of a harsh voice from the doorway pulled her up short.

"Back off, Shaeffer. It's obvious the lady doesn't want anything to do with you . . . or your bed."

"Derek!" Cathy cried. "What . . . how . . ."

"The front door was open. And the loudness of your

little spat didn't exactly leave me in any mystery as to your whereabouts."

"Look, Guenther," Syd said in a nasty, guttural tone tinged with anger, "*you* back off. You're the one who isn't wanted here . . . ever. After the way you treated Cathy at that party, in front of all those people, I'm surprised you dare show your face in this house."

Derek's eyes were narrowed and the muscle in his jaw was twitching ominously. Instinctively then, Cathy moved to position herself between the two men. She raised her hands.

"Stop it, both of you. My uncle is very sick . . . very! I don't want any kind of a scene in this house—not for myself and certainly not one that would disturb him!" She turned to Syd. "I'll discuss all this with you later." She turned to Derek. "And as for you, just why are you here, here of all places, anyway?"

"Why do you think? You wouldn't answer my calls. You're hiding out in this house. It seemed the only way to get to you was to come to your lair."

There was heavy sarcasm in that last word and Cathy reacted with bitterness. "As it happens, I was going to get in touch with you tomorrow." Her chin trembled. She felt torn, not knowing which of these angry men she should deal with first . . . or how to handle them both at the same time. "Why don't you both go and just leave me alone?" she sighed heavily.

"Not on your life," Derek snarled. "Not until I've seen the back of that weak-chinned friend of yours."

"Why, you bastard," Syd choked, heading fast for Derek, virtually hurling Cathy out of his way.

There was a fight in the making. A fight over her. Cathy recoiled, horrified. "Stop it!" she shouted hoarsely. "Stop it!"

They were shoving each other, rather like school-boys in a scuffle in the playground, and had backed into the front hall. Cathy was right behind them, prepared to throw herself between them to put an end to this nonsensical farce. And then a quiet voice on the staircase froze all three of them into a tableau of distorted figures. It was Mr. Franklin who spoke.

"Miss Cathy," he called a second time, gently, and ignoring the men, "he's gone. Your uncle has just passed away not more than a few minutes ago."

She had known, of course. Known. But it made no difference—not the least difference...because the reality was different than the anticipation. And she'd thought there'd be more *time*. Time for her to sit beside him and reminisce, read to him, care for him. Only her gasp of shock sounded in the stillness.

"I've called for the doctor and the ambulance...you know, the funeral home ambulance," Mr. Franklin said. When Cathy didn't reply, didn't even move, he added, "the authorities require a death certificate from the doctor and I...well, I thought it would be best to have the...well, I thought we'd all feel better having his body removed as soon as the ambulance can get here from Blantyre."

All the responsibility rested on her now, Cathy realized, and she quickly drew herself up to meet it. "Yes, of course. You've done just the right things, Mr. Franklin. Thank you." She glanced at Derek and

Syd. "Under the circumstances, I'm sure you'll give up this foolishness and be good enough to leave." Then, with withering scorn, she added, "Neither of you is wanted or needed here now."

Both of them protested, of course. Both wanted to stay to help. But firmly she denied them and firmly she ushered them out.

The funeral was held three days later in Blantyre, in an old church her uncle had loved and sometimes attended. Cathy knew her uncle loathed traditional funerals as much as she—closed rooms filled with the cloying smell from stiff floral wreaths, the constant droning of organ music, the insincere words from people who'd barely known the deceased. She arranged the service for him—"the guest of honor"—as he would have loved and appreciated it. She had wild flowers and grasses, many of them from Tanyasi's acres. Soft native music made by Nyanja tribesmen who'd known and appreciated her uncle filled the church. And the eulogies were delivered by people who'd truly liked Howard and his life's work. There was the veterinarian who'd been so close to the Tanyasi preservation project; a government official with whom he'd worked for years on coordinating his plans with the wider plans made for wildlife throughout Malawi. These were two of her uncle's oldest and best friends and their words were profound and meaningful. Cathy spoke briefly, too, and when the service was over she felt a deep sense of peace and contentment . . . overlaying her feeling of loss.

Greeting people outdoors under an old and gnarled knobthorn tree, Cathy was impressed with the numbers of people who had driven great distances on short notice to attend the funeral. At the last there was Mrs. Windon. Cathy was surprised to see her. She was dressed, typically, in an elegant somber gray suit. Her only jewelry was a single strand of fine baroque pearls.

"My dear," Mrs. Windon said, "I hope you are bearing up all right."

"Why, yes, certainly, I am."

"But you are wondering why I'm here, aren't you?"

Cathy nodded. "Frankly, I didn't expect to see anyone from the Guenther family at this funeral. You're welcome, though, of course."

"That's good of you." She replied. "And thank you. I might as well tell you—I didn't come here today to pay my last respects. I came here simply and solely for the purpose of forcing myself to forgive Howard."

Cathy frowned, suddenly eager to make the woman understand her uncle's side of the years' old bitterness between their families. "My uncle told me a number of things before he died. I'm sure they're true . . . under the circumstances."

Mrs. Windon glanced around. Most of the mourners were drifting away. Only a few remained by their cars waiting to accompany the hearse the great distance— all the way back to Tanyasi—to the site Cathy had chosen for her uncle's burial place.

"This isn't the moment to talk. But we really must. Afterward, perhaps?"

She nodded slowly. "Certainly. A few people will be coming to Africa House after the burial." She glanced at her watch. "They should be gone by tea time. Will you drop in then?"

"I'd be glad to." She put out a hand to detain Cathy. "Would you mind if I went along to the—"

"No, not at all. Why don't you follow our car? I'll be riding with the Franklins."

Mrs. Windon kissed her cheek and they parted then.

It was after four when the guests left and Mrs. Windon joined Cathy in the living room for their talk.

"What a lovely spot you selected as a resting place for Howard," Mrs. Windon began. "I know everyone has told you, but still I had to add my own appreciation. Just perfect for a lover of wildlife, a person devoted to its preservation."

"Thank you," Cathy murmured, her eyes misted with tears as the picture of the little grove, far from the house, came to mind. It was surrounded with acacias and boasted a large moss-covered boulder. It was a tranquil nook in the Tanyasi acreage and one she and her uncle had visited often in her youth. They both loved the spot.

Cathy pulled herself back to the present and eyed Mrs. Windon levelly.

"I know about the partnership between my uncle and Derek's father. I know it went sour. My uncle told me, along with the fact that Pieter, if I may call him by his first name, had problems . . . personal problems, weaknesses."

"Yes of course that's part of it," replied Mrs. Windon softly. "Pieter did have terrible problems, great personal weaknesses."

Cathy went on, straining to be tactful yet honest. "Everything between Derek's father and my uncle happened unintentionally. It was all a string of horrible coincidences, even down to the very last when Uncle Howard had bought Tanyasi, not knowing who it used to belong to."

Mrs. Windon frowned but said nothing as Cathy leaned to her, reached for her hand and squeezed it. "He told me this... he practically swore it to me just a short time before he died." She met the other woman's eyes and held them with her own. "I know uncle would want to apologize for the grief he unwittingly caused your family. He can't, so I'll have to do it for him. I'm truly sorry, and I hope in time all the bitterness can be dispelled. But you must believe what happened *was* unintentional!"

Mrs. Windon looked thoughtful, dubious. As she remained silent, Cathy rushed on.

"What my uncle never explained was why Derek's father was so bitterly determined to believe he wanted to ruin him. I mean, my uncle should have been able to make him see how all those things that happened were just accidental. Your brother's worst fears had no basis in truth. A reasonable man would at least have listened. Why didn't Pieter listen? Was he insane as well as bitter?"

The woman shook her head. "No, he was flawed, but not out of his mind. He had good reason for believing as he did."

"Reason? What reason?" Cathy asked urgently.

Mrs. Windon seemed reluctant to answer. "If your uncle never told you, perhaps I shouldn't either.

Maybe I should respect the dead in what seem to be his last wishes."

Cathy's eyes blazed. "He didn't have time...or opportunity there at the end. *Please*! I feel I *have* to know."

"I guess it can't hurt. They're all dead now." Mrs. Windon shrugged and sighed. "Cathy, your uncle loved Derek's mother. He and my brother both wanted to marry her. In the end she chose Pieter over Howard. Later on I think she regretted her choice, but by then of course it was too late. Divorce wasn't common in those days, nor as socially acceptable as it is now. In any case, with his drinking and gambling Pieter couldn't have been a very satisfactory husband." She blinked hard. Cathy could see the subject of Pieter was terribly painful.

"Later," Mrs. Windon went on, "when your uncle ended up with much of my brother's lost wealth—and his home as well—it was only natural for Pieter to believe Howard had gone out of his way to ruin him. It seemed less than coincidence to any of us that none of this occurred until after Elizabeth, Derek's mother, died. Right or wrong it seemed as if Howard waited, biding his time until he could lash back at Pieter without hurting Elizabeth. Unfortunately, if such was truly the case, he did not stop to think that by ruining Pieter he was also hurting Elizabeth's son."

"Hurt Derek? Hurt a small boy? I can't and won't believe that of my uncle. I trust what he told me. I trust that all that happened, all that he did was done unwittingly."

The woman shrugged. "But of course we don't know for sure. Maybe it *was* as Howard claimed—purely a string of horrible coincidences. For the sake of Howard's soul, I hope so, but in any case, Pieter believed otherwise. And, oh, he believed it with all his heart and soul . . . and his belief carried all the rest of us along with him."

Cathy could only stare. It all fit—the angry bitterness toward Derek's father and family. It made sense. With a pang she wondered if her uncle had loved at all the woman he had finally married. Did all this explain the lines of dissatisfaction she had noticed, even as a child, around Aunt Mary's mouth? She cringed. She *wanted* to believe her uncle. She didn't want even to suspect he knowingly set out to ruin his rival in love. She preferred to believe that her uncle was innocent, or at worst that the truth rested somewhere between the extreme positions held by both men.

"Oh, but surely after you knew about Derek's father and fully realized what he was like," Cathy said, "you'd have known my uncle wasn't necessarily to blame."

"Family loyalties override everything," Mrs. Windon said staunchly. "Years passed. The family became separated, and indifference to this affair began to set in. When I ended up with little Derek after Pieter went off the deep end, I did my best to help him rid himself of the hatreds his early training had drummed into him. Fortunately, because of Derek's basic nature, this proved quite easy to accomplish. Of course Derek never warmed to Howard, especially after he started going around with you and knew Howard had forbidden it."

Cathy smiled a little ruefully. "Especially then," she murmured. She remembered the stormy scenes between her uncle and the handsome wild youth Derek had been in those years. "In all fairness, my uncle never really warmed to Derek either. He never trusted him. Certainly he didn't want him hanging around me. I suppose under the circumstances it's no wonder they both stayed so hostile toward one another."

Derek! Anguish raked her insides like metal teeth gouging flesh. Derek! "Derek hates me," she said in a voice hoarse with pain. "He despises me just as did his entire family. He only 'cultivated' me to get back at my uncle by hurting me."

Mrs. Windon smiled, but sadly. "Oh, but my dear, it is *you* who are mistaken there!" She went on with sudden intensity. "Derek knows—he understands— that love is more important than a family feud. Love warms and nourishes. Hate only chills and withers. Unfortunately," she added, shrugging, "those two passions are often sadly confused."

But her uncle's words haunted Cathy. "He—he hated my family...and everyone in it. His father taught him to and he displayed it more than once."

"Cathy, Cathy, he outgrew all that years ago. It was true what he was like as a child. My brother—" Mrs. Windon spread her hands in a gesture of resignation. "As you so delicately put it, my brother, rest his tortured soul, had problems, flaws in his character. He was obsessed with hatred for your uncle. He blamed Howard, probably unfairly, for his own failure. And yes, he taught his only child to hate, but don't you see? No matter how hard Pieter tried, he couldn't change the wholesome kernel of Derek's personality. As a child, Derek hated because of the way he was taught, but to believe he carried that with him throughout his later life was a terrible mistake your uncle made and now you're making. As soon as he was old enough to understand and think for himself, Derek rejected all that old poison. He had no revenge in his heart. I know, because I helped raise him. I know Derek as well as anyone."

"But—but he always spoke so harshly about my uncle. Certainly he seemed to have hated him."

The woman shrugged. "Derek has always been strong-willed with a good sense of his own worth. He encountered a man who treated him unpleasantly whenever they met and even forbade him from seeing the girl he truly cared about. I'm not saying it's right, but it was natural that my nephew fought back. That doesn't mean he hated Howard, only that he resented what he believed to be Howard's unfairness."

Cathy knew that suspicion showed on her face; it certainly sounded in her voice as she echoed Mrs. Windon's words. "The one girl he truly cared about? I sincerely doubt that given the way he's behaved recently. And, after all, he is—" She broke off, unwilling to mention Mina.

"Cathy, out of all the women my nephew has ever known...and he has known many," she added with a note of amused regret, "you have affected him most strongly. You alone have been able to arouse him to rage. You've led him to grief more than once and even to moments of tenderness that border embarrassingly on the mawkish."

Cathy blinked, disbelieving.

"Doesn't that tell you *anything*?" Mrs. Windon asked wryly. "Or rather, doesn't that tell you *everything*?"

chapter 15

WHEN WAS ONE moment born, Cathy wondered, and when did another die? Time now was marked by distance traveled. The car wheels revolved, each turn taking Cathy farther from Africa House and closer to a meeting she knew held the seeds of her destiny.

The evening had brought mist, then occasional drizzle. The indecisiveness of the weather matched her own mood. Everything was veiled in gray and was sometimes attractive and promising, sometimes dreary and threatening. There was a small shower and she turned on the windshield wipers. They swished back and forth in a jarringly squeaky, yet hypnotizing rhythm. With a pang she remembered the rain those few days past . . . those eons ago. And, of course, the man to whom she was driving and with whom she'd shared those hours in the rain. *And* with whom she'd spent so many hours six years before.

The picture of Mina Van Ness burst into her mind and she shuddered. How had such a woman come to be born to one of the local landowners? And how had Derek been ensnared by her? He was so down-to-earth, so real . . . or he *had* been, she reminded herself.

Her mind spun on the matter of time . . . time passing. Wasn't that the crux of the grave problem she faced in terms of her feelings for Derek? He could be a stranger now; she certainly wasn't the same young woman who'd parted from him when the accident had occured—although her body had reacted on first encounter again with Derek as though not an hour had passed since she was twenty and completely, madly, tempestuously in love with him. She'd reverted to immaturity in every meeting with him, with every sight of him since . . .

She bit her lip in consternation. "My God!" she said fiercely under her breath. What if she couldn't control herself now with him. She shook her head in self-reproach. Nonsense! Even with all the pressure and strain she knew she had—at last—got a grip on herself where Derek was concerned.

His lodge was visible through the trees. She stepped on the accelerator, forgetting she'd left the bitumenized road and was on one of the lesser graveled byways. The fine stones mixed with sand splattered in wide arcs to either side of the car. She laughed aloud then and slowed the car. Cathy-the-jinx-with-a-car! That's what Derek had called her. She dared not be anything but careful easing up the incline to the space adjacent to his kitchen door where Angus Mac-Dowell's friends had waited while the three prepared to go off with them during the flood. She yanked on the emergency brake and glanced warily toward the door. Her heart began to pound heavily...especially when she saw Derek walk around the house. He stopped a few yards away, hands rising to his waist and eyed her narrowly. She swallowed hard and got out of the car.

"Hello," she called, but it was a tentative, quavering sound.

He said nothing, letting her pick her way self-consciously to him. She halted in front of him. There was a breathless quality to those long moments when they held one another's eyes.

He nodded curtly, breaking the spell of paralyzed silence that cocooned them. "Why *here*, Cathy? Here of all places?" His voice was low, full of emotion.

"I asked for our meeting here because I simply felt Africa House was wrong...alien to you...and I didn't know any other place to suggest."

Derek's brows rose, but Cathy couldn't figure out whether from skepticism or a sort of wry appreciation of her being considerate about his coming to her in her uncle's house. She took a steadying breath. "As I briefly mentioned on the phone, Derek, I asked to see you because I learned a lot from my uncle before his death and also because—"

"Let's go inside," Derek interrupted, eyes burning

hotly into hers. "Unless you object and want to stand outside!"

She cleared her throat. "No, I mean, yes. I'd like to go inside." Damn! His very presence was getting her off-balance again.

Derek had rearranged the modular units so that their black shapes no longer resembled at all the forms they'd been in on that night of the awful scene between them. So, she thought, it wasn't only she who was conscious of the embarrassments, the bad memories of the other. She smiled secretly.

"Drink?" he asked, indicating with a wave of his hand that she take a seat near the fireplace.

"Uh, no. I . . . I'd just like a talk."

"That's not what I'd like," he growled.

Her eyes flew to his face. She didn't know if he wanted to beat her or make love to her. His expression was thunderously clouded with emotion. Instinctively she raised her hand as if to ward off a blow.

"Please," she said, beseeching him with her eyes to hold his hot feelings in check. "We really *must* settle so much between us. Only then will we be free . . ."

"Cathy," he said in a voice of exquisite softness, "we are free. I know all about your conversation with my aunt. Apparently you have only to believe that I wasn't filled with hatred for your uncle." His voice trailed off. He went tense all of a sudden.

Cathy was mesmerized by the look in Derek's eyes, the lines on his face. She gasped, then chewed on her lip. Feelings of tenderness and love washed over her.

How she loved this man. She knew the strangest sense of yearning and realized with a start that more than anything she wanted to live the rest of her life with him, have his children. Tears started in her eyes.

"Ahh, Cathy," Derek crooned. His arms shot out to wrap her, then fold her against his broad chest and rock her gently. "You're so alive," he whispered, "so passionate and emotional, darling girl."

She was trembling, her blood coursing through her veins. She longed for his kiss, his passion. Sharply, horrifyingly, she remembered Mina and dragged herself out of Derek's embrace. She leaped to her feet and paced far away from him.

"What the hell?" he said, shocked.

But Cathy was thinking furiously. What was Derek doing? Consoling an old childhood sweetheart who'd lost her close relative and seen him buried? He might still cherish her even, want to protect her, but perhaps he was only savoring what had been—not what could be.

"Perhaps I made a mistake," she said at last. "You probably want to be with your fiancée."

"Fiancée?" Derek asked incredulously.

"Yes," she drawled, "your darling, precious Mina."

He was on his feet and across the room in front of her in the wink of an eye. His arms shot out, his hands reaching for her shoulders, holding her painfully.

"Let me go, damn it!" Cathy cried, suddenly angry.

"Never. Mina is *not* my precious anything, you little fool. I don't love Mina."

"You could have fooled me!" she retorted. "I suppose you went driving with her the other day just because you enjoy her delightful company."

"I don't find her company at all delightful," he said quickly. He was clearly exasperated. "And I was driving her to the hospital. Her father had a heart attack and she needed a ride to follow him there. She had left her own car in Johannesburg when she flew in to visit. Mina just doesn't know how to drive any of her papa's stick shift cars."

Startled, Cathy drew back, then turned around to stare at him. "To the hospital?" She remembered suddenly that she had seen an ambulance pass her by on the road.

"Yes, to the hospital. Now get something straight. Mina and I went out together a few times while I lived in Johannesburg, but I never promised her anything. Nevertheless she had set her cap for me. I guess she thought my income and mining interests would keep her in the style to which she was accustomed, or would like to become accustomed, but I had other ideas. I don't go for the big-city type girl anyway and so when I left to return home, I thought I had seen the last of her. Imagine my surprise," he added grimly, "when she turned up in Malawi again, evidently following after me. I only drove her to the hospital as a favor. I'd have done it for anyone."

He smiled at her, but in his eyes she caught an odd glitter. "Oh, Cathy, when you showed up at my aunt's party with that jerk Syd, I was furious. I couldn't believe you'd do it, not after all that had gone on between us in the cave...before. Then you started

waving that damned bracelet in my face, and I swear
I saw red. I could have murdered you—and him, too."

"Syd," she murmured. "My Lord, I'd forgotten all
about him, about taking care of settling—"

Derek burst in on her words, laughing. "I've taken
care of him. Don't you worry. He already knows something you don't know."

Her eyes widened. "Really?"

"Really!" He grinned and pulled her close for a
long, lingering hot kiss. Cathy went weak and would
have fallen when he released her if she weren't still
in the supportive circle of his arms.

"Cathy, my foolish darling, I love you with all my
heart, my soul, my body. We're both pigheaded, I'm
afraid. Too strong-willed also. But that doesn't stop
me from wanting you forever and for always. We
parted six years ago when we shouldn't have. I'm
never going to let anyone interfere with us again. Do
you understand?"

Cathy was too thrilled for words. She nodded
meekly. Her pulse rate was soaring with his every
word . . . every word she knew she'd wanted to hear
all through these last dreary years away from him, the
man she loved fiercely.

"Cathy," he murmured, "I've never loved anyone
as I love you."

His eyes seemed to devour her. They feasted for a
moment upon her face, gazing deep into her own, then
dropped low to her breasts. His hand reached out to
cup one tender mound from below. His face was trans-
fixed with love. She gazed fascinated, her eyes wide

and wondering. Her heart pounded wildly. All her old desire burst once again into raging, flaming life. Trembling in his arms with flesh alive and vibrant to his touch, she ached for Derek to press lips upon her everywhere, to claim her with his passion.

"Oh, Derek, Derek!" Cathy buried her face in his shirt.

A swelling heat pulsed deep inside her. Her flesh seemed to scorch and burn where it touched his, but pleasantly so. No other man had ever satisfied her the way Derek did and could. Clinging to him, drawing close, she knew only Derek could bring her the true satisfaction and joy she craved.

"Derek, I love you more than I can say. You must know that."

He laughed with delight and stroked her hair. "There's only one way to cut through the tangled messes we always make—"

"One way? What do you mean?" She was flooded with a thrilling anxiety that almost took her breath away.

"I want us to drive back to Blantyre, *right now*. We're going to find someone to marry us tonight."

"Marry..." Tears welled in Cathy's eyes.

"I've always loved you," Derek said tenderly. "There have been other women since you, but none of them ever satisfied me. I tried to convince myself I hated you, that I'd only courted you because of your uncle and the feud between our families. What nonsense. You, Cathy, you. I could never get you out of my system. I never will get you out of my system."

"Oh, Derek, my uncle never really hated you. He distrusted you. He believed you were just using me to get back at him."

"Damn!" Derek cried. "And because of all that we've been kept from each other these years."

"Please," she murmured tenderly. "That's all in the past. We're going to be married now, remember?"

"How could I forget, my darling, my love?" Derek kissed her gently on the lips, but the kiss deepened. It was the rapture they'd known long ago and would know again and again. It was hard won, but it was gained and it would last. There was no doubting it now. Their love would last their lifetime through.

Introducing a unique new concept in romance novels!
Every woman deserves a...

Second Chance at Love ™

You'll revel in the settings, you'll delight
in the heroines, you may even fall in love with the
magnetic men you meet in the pages of...

SECOND CHANCE AT LOVE

Look for three new
novels of lovers lost and found coming every
month from Jove! Available now:

_____05703-7	FLAMENCO NIGHTS (#1) by Susanna Collins	$1.75
_____05637-5	WINTER LOVE SONG (#2) by Meredith Kingston	$1.75
_____05624-3	THE CHADBOURNE LUCK (#3) by Lucia Curzon	$1.75
_____05777-0	OUT OF A DREAM (#4) by Jennifer Rose	$1.75
_____05878-5	GLITTER GIRL (#5) by Jocelyn Day	$1.75
_____05863-7	AN ARTFUL LADY (#6) by Sabina Clark	$1.75
_____05694-4	EMERALD BAY (#7) by Winter Ames	$1.75
_____05776-2	RAPTURE REGAINED (#8) by Serena Alexander	$1.75
_____05801-7	THE CAUTIOUS HEART (#9) by Philippa Heywood	$1.75

Available at your local bookstore or return this form to:

J JOVE/BOOK MAILING SERVICE
P.O. Box 690, Rockville Center, N.Y. 11570

**Please enclose 50¢ for postage and handling for one book, 25¢
each add'l book ($1.25 max.). No cash, CODs or stamps. Total
amount enclosed: $_____ in check or money order.**

NAME_____

ADDRESS_____

CITY_____STATE/ZIP_____

Allow three weeks for delivery.   SK-13